T0322480

Icelandic Folk Tales

Hjörleifur Helgi Stefánsson

The History Press

Cover illustrations: © ???
Illustrated by Tord Sandström Fahlström
"Ethnic" icons by Evgeni Moryakov, from thenounproject.com.

First published 2021
Reprinted 2023

The History Press
97 St George's Place,
Cheltenham,
Gloucestershire,
GL50 3QB
www.thehistorypress.co.uk

British Library Cataloguing in Publication Data.
A catalogue record for this book is available from the British Library.

ISBN 978 0 7509 9314 2

Typesetting and origination by Typo•glyphix, Burton-on-Trent
Printed and bound by Thomson Press, India

Contents

o>IIII><

Introduction and Acknowledgements

To sit down and write a handful of one's favourite tales is a wondrous task. Too much coffee and the river view out of our living room window in the midst of winter creates just the right atmosphere to lure out my ancestors, whether they be people, trolls, ghosts or what have you. It happens to be the same view I had growing up with my parents, Ragnheiður and Stefán. My father rebuilt and added to the house built by my mother's grandfather to make room for all of us and my mother grew up on the same farm as me and my siblings and probably did every single awful thing herself that we then later got told off for. I know for a fact that she used to take the milk from the farm on the 1954 International Harvester D217 to meet the collecting lorry, and when out of view she would take it up to sixth gear and full speed. She got caught when she tipped it over one day and probably got a word in her ear, as we say. Is it any wonder us kids grew up to become such hooligans? One of the things I see out the window, just a stone's throw away, is Ánabrekka, the house of my late grandparents, Ása and Jóhannes. As I was growing up I spent just as much time on their farm as I did on ours, which is not strange at all considering the two are roughly a kilometre apart. To grow up with one's grandparents is a true privilege and mine were incredible people. They were born in the old time, in the old country, and they gave me, in my upbringing, a glimpse of another way of thinking and living. Their focus was on people and tradition, they were incredibly hard working and they loved unconditionally. Being very different, they each gave me their own lesson on the past. To their memory I dedicate this first collection of mine.

Amma was a tough lady. She was born in a house of turf and stone and knew hardship. She also knew toil and loss from a very young age and maybe that was somewhat reflected in the way she lived her life. To some, she seemed rough and distant and perhaps she was, but a hard shell is needed for a life that can be cold as a raging snowstorm. Underneath was the open and warm heart of an artist, one that could make anything grow in her garden and one that created the best and beautiful garments to keep her children warm and safe and I got to be one of them. Travelling was her passion and as a grown woman she saw faraway lands, with Asia being the love of her life. She taught me to do my tasks well and question authority, and she taught me to always be myself – I might have lost that fellow at some point but she set me straight with what she had given me to work with. She made me promise I would never become a politician. She was wise and I miss her.

Afi saw our ancestors in a beam of light and made sure I knew them well, he was third generation on our farmland and was very proud of that fact. He believed the land should be worked, a farmer by nature and nurture who tended his animals well and spoke to himself all day long. I even heard a row one morning as he drank his coffee alone in his study. That must have been about something very important. He recited poetry day in and day out and was the most knowledgeable person I have ever known. He was a brilliant angler who knew his river like the back of his hand and was a friend of the salmon. His horses were grey and tall and he was never happier then when he rode through the highlands of the west gathering sheep with his friends and fellow farmers and a flask in his pocket. He gave me my love of tales and the land that they grew from; some of the first stories I remember reading came from books he either gave me or made sure I read. He was a true scholar and I miss him.

Living on a farm with a river running past it, horses to ride in the stables, all sorts of trucks and tractors at hand, a loving family and brilliant storytellers all around are the perfect surroundings to create oneself. Stories are born and shared every day and need to be told in order for them to exist. My parents are without a doubt the best storytellers I have heard and that is saying something, as I am lucky enough to be friends with some of the very best. It was not until I met my brother of lore, Tom Muir of Orkney, that I knew there was such a thing as a storyteller. He has taught me what little I know about delivering a story; I proudly hold the title 'Pet Viking' and I do not think there are many others who do. Without him it is quite possible that no one would sit through my ramblings or read my gibberish. Lawrence Tulloch had a great impact on me, a wonderful man and a master storyteller, I miss him dearly and his books are an inspiration for me to write. Jerker Fahlström, my beloved sea ghost brother who teaches me about Scandinavian lore and my boys to fight with a sword, is another master at the trade, and so is Ruth Kirkpatrick, who puts some sort of magic in her tales of ancestry and hidden beings. Dr Donald Smith took a chance years ago and put an Icelandic kid on his stage with some of the best performers in the world and then, he did it again! My siblings, my friends, my children and my youngsters keep me in practice as they are my audience whenever I am bursting with a story. My dearest Anna has patience and makes everything possible. I love you. Those are the people that make me who I am today and for that I am thankful.

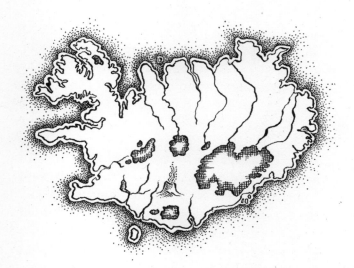

The Snuffbox

A while back, in fact quite a long while back when the people of Iceland lived under turf scattered about like sheep grazing, there lived a man by the name of Jón. He lived in an area of Iceland named Snæfellsnes, a windswept peninsula that reaches far out into the Atlantic Ocean. The strong waves there hammer the jet-black beaches and jagged cliffs mercilessly, shaping the land and the people that have lived there for generations. In days of old the people of Snæfellsnes were hardened, perhaps even rough people, that brought their livelihood from the sea in open boats of eight rowers in all weathers. The sea took its toll though; many were lost to the deep over the centuries, many good men did not return to their families after a rough dance with King Ægir.

Our friend Jón, however, had a different way of making a living, though. Sure, he had been at sea for years and he had worked all the jobs on the small farms, whose tiny turf houses dotted the slopes along the shores like mounds from the earth. But now a fully grown man, he made his own living. Some years back, he had been the first to arrive at a stranded ship one stormy night and had helped the Dutch fishermen escape their broken up schooner to the safety of a nearby farm. He was as strong as an ox, he was, and courageous like a troll in the mountains, and one by one he brought the sailors through the fierce waves to the shore with the wind howling and screaming and snow whirling from every direction till he finally brought the captain last to safety. As a gift of gratitude, when the captain and the crew had gathered their strength, they gave him something quite unique, a flintlock shotgun they had managed to salvage from the wreck of their ship along with a huge, wax-sealed trunk full of pellets and powder. This was very much against the law at the time; the Dutch and the French fished the Icelandic waters all around the country and to make sure the local merchants could continue getting rich selling maggoty meal and Brennivín (our oh so lovely and strong local schnaps), the law forbade Icelanders having any dealings with the foreign fishermen. For some reason though, the babies in certain areas round the country began to be born with a darker shade than before, but no one knows how that could have come to be. Our Jón had never been too worried about the authorities and gladly accepted the good gift from the grateful captain, becoming the first man in Snæfellsnes to own a gun.

This led to Jón finding a new and better way to make a living. He travelled on foot from farm to farm with his trusted weapon round his shoulder and shot birds from the cliffs rising from the sea, providing fresh meat for the farmers and their families as well as keeping foxes away from the down-filled nests of the eider duck. For this he accepted butter and meat, money and crafts, skins and favours and everything in between.

⌖⋙⋘⌖

His reputation grew and he became known for his gun and his courage.

One particularly dreary and foggy night, Jón was making his way from one farm to the next where he had been asked to get rid of a particularly stubborn fox that was eating away all the eggs of the eider. He was walking a very narrow footpath he had walked often before, on his left hand was a sheer drop onto the jagged cliffs and the sea below and on his right stretched a vertical mountain side up to the heavens above. As he made his way, he felt a sudden cold, an eerie and even colder gust of wind than the night was blowing his way and a shudder crawled over his shoulders. Out there in the fog he saw a very big shape taking form in front of him and, thinking of the faraway possibility of an ice bear wandering off the land-locked ice the previous winter, he ran his fingers along the shaft of his gun beside him. On he walked, nowhere to go but onward, and soon saw the shape of a huge man emerging fully from the thick fog. He was briefly relieved, but soon saw that this was no ordinary man. The man in front of him was wearing tattered and oilskin clothes, water seeping from under the sleeves, no shoes to protect mangled, bloody feet. In fact, the man seemed drenched and hurt as he had just fallen overboard and fought for his life on the shores below. It was at that moment it dawned on Jón what he was facing there on the steep mountainside. Not only was he faced with a ghost, but a sea ghost, the ghost of a man who had drowned at sea and never been laid to the long sleep of the hallowed ground. Those were the fiercest of all ghosts, Jón knew very well from the countless tales he had heard in his upbringing, tales of struggles in dark nights, broken bones and even death.

He prepared himself for a fight, knowing very well that he had but one chance and one chance only to defeat that dark being and get away with his life. Turning back was not an option; no one runs from a ghost, not any more than we run from our fate. The ghost stepped a few paces nearer, the stench of death reaching Jón's nose and, to Jón's amazement, and not at all calming in any way, he spoke!

'Whaaat do you haaave haaanging there?'

The ghost grunted in a deep voice and pointed at Jón's belt. Jón looked down and saw that the ghost was pointing at a hollowed-out ram's horn that held the powder for the shotgun. Traditionally such hollowed out horns were used, and in fact still are, as snuffboxes. This particular horn was so big that Jón had taken to keeping his gunpowder in it rather than his snuff. Thinking so fast and so hard he could hear his own brain cracking, he looked upon the endlessly tall ghost and said, 'Why, it's my snuffbox. And this ...' he grabbed his gun from behind his back, 'this is the tool we use nowadays to get the snuff up our noses. Would you like some snuff?'

The ghost looked sternly at Jón and then replied, 'Aye, I liked my snuff when I lived and haven't had some for a hundred years.'

At this, Jón took a step back and poured a generous trickle of powder down the barrel of his gun. He then, turning his back slightly to the curious-looking ghost, grabbed a handful of pellets and ran those down the barrel as well. He now pointed the gun up the ghost's nostrils and fired. BOOM! The loud bang echoed from the cliffs around them and rang in Jón's ears as a thick cloud of smoke and fog swallowed the pair of them. Jón stepped back, gazing at the ghost, and heard a strong spit.

Again, he prepared for a fight, as it dawned on him that he had probably made the last mistake of his life, angering a sea ghost in the middle of the night, all alone on a treacherous mountain path. As he watched the thick smoke slowly vanishing he saw the ghost with his face down, loudly spitting out the generous amount of unburst powder and pellets Jón had given him. With a look of utter satisfaction, the ghost beamed at Jón and said, 'Now that was some proper snuff.' With that and a crooked, toothless smile on his face, the ghost passed Jón and was swallowed by the darkness.

This was the first and last time Jón was bothered by a ghost, in fact he lived to a ripe old age and luck followed him through all his paths in life. From him comes a strong line of hard-working and intelligent people that have made their fortune in all sorts of manner, now spread around our island in the north. And how, you might wonder, do I know all this to such detail? Well, you see, my grandmother, who was a warm-hearted, clever and strong woman who spoke her mind without nonsense, was born on a small farm called Geirakot in Snæfellsnes. She was, of course, one of Jón's descendants.

Of Ghosts

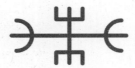

The history of ghosts in Iceland is as long as our own, and our relationship with them is complicated, to say the least. From ghosts of newborns left to die who terrorise the mother to skinless, raging bulls, the entities can be as different as they are many. The long and dark winters gave us endless tales of ghosts of women, men, animals and even the ghosts of still living people, who bode nothing good for the one who met those or saw them. Ours is a dark country in the winter, to say the least. In the time when ghosts followed our every footstep (who is to say they don't even still?) we lived scattered around the country in farms and small fishing villages and darkness was thick. Lighting was very minimal, simple lamps with cotton grass wicks burned fish liver oil and gave off more smell than light, as candles were a real luxury. Paraffin lamps were introduced much later and changed the atmosphere of the houses dramatically.

We were born in our homes and we died there, events that now are very much hidden away from us, especially the latter. When a person died in the old country, numerous customs were honoured to make sure the deceased stayed that way. One of them was to wash and clothe the body in linen, another was to have a member of the household wake over the body, and yet another one was not to carry the body out the main door, which in some cases meant that a hole had to be torn in a wall of turf and stone, in order to get them to the grave. These habits, however, were not always sufficient, since the fear of ghosts was embedded in us. A common greeting, when a knock was heard upon a door, or someone seen in the dark being, 'Be you living or dead?' People travelled heaths and mountain roads in dark and dreary weather and got lost and died frequently, an event we simply call 'to remain outside'. These were often the less fortunate, the poor, the drifters, single mothers and the handicapped. And indeed many of those who perished on their way between farms or over a mountain road in the dead of winter remained outside, remained as ghosts, who terrorised the living, bound to the place where they froze to death, alone or even with a toddler in their arms.

It is therefore, perhaps, no wonder that ghosts are embedded in our culture and lore. When my mother first visited my father's stomping grounds, he led her around his small village and told her a ghost story at every turn. She looked at him with a smile and said something the likes of 'the way you tell it, one might think the whole village was cramped with ghosts my dear', and with a look of surprise my father replied, 'Well, what you have to understand is that it is.' Another classic setting for a haunting is, of course, the graveyard, which has given us many tales of struggles in the dead of night, churches full of corpses and young women being lured into open graves. A family graveyard sits next to our farmhouse and has been in use for generations now, however, the graves in there remain firmly closed and calm.

As one might expect, graveyards and ghosts connect strongly with the practice of magic. Dark, indeed, very dark things are connected with the dead and the dying, such as the famous 'nábrækur' or necropants. They are, in fact, not that hard to create, should you be interested. All you have to do is to make a deal with a man for his corpse, upon his death. You will then dig him up, after the funeral, and flay him from the waist down and immediately put on the newly created pants. They will then heal on to your flesh. You will then place a coin, stolen from a poor widow, in the scrotum of the pants and that will attract more coins. That scrotum will never be empty and you become rich. Make sure, however, that you have found someone to inherit the pants before you die, or you will go barking mad to your death.

Another thing that might come in handy one day is to have your own ghost. Simply do as follows. Find a fresh grave and walk around it counterclockwise, round and round and round. Recite specific, awful poetry (travel to Iceland and do your research) as you increase your speed and intensity. A hand should now emerge from the topsoil, followed by an arm, a shoulder, a head, etc. Once you have summoned the corpse out of the grave you have to attack it with all your might. And you have to win. If you lose, you will be dragged into the grave to spend eternity next to someone you do not even know, or worse, someone you do not particularly like. Assuming that you have won the fight, and have the ghost pinned down on the grave, all you have to do now is to lick and drink the mucus and blood foam around its mouth, and you have yourself a ghost. Use wisely.

Herding Mice

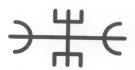

Straumfjörður is a magical place. It is a fjord in west Iceland with yellow sandy beaches and hundreds of skerries (small, rocky islands) in the waters, some visible, others lurking just below the surface at high tide. It is home to seals and seabirds in their thousands, incredible nature and good people. Those skerries have claimed a hefty toll through the ages as Straumfjörður was settled a long time ago and those who have lived there have both rowed and sailed in all weathers as a part of their daily life and survival. Very good fishing grounds are outside of the fjord and trout swims between the skerries in spring. The land way to the farmstead is long and very boggy, and on top of that flooded during high tide as the farm sits on an island. This remarkable place was a merchant site for the rural area of Mýrar from the seventeenth century, with big vessels from Denmark making port in a strait formed by an island just off the coast. Ruins of great houses line the beach along the strait to this day and tell the often grim story of the relationship between humble farm folk and the wealthy and sometimes ruthless merchant class.

A grand villa was built there in the nineteenth century to house a store and the merchant's family, but was taken apart and moved to serve as a rectory when the trade moved to the town of Borgarnes.

Long before any of that, there lived a fine woman in Straumfjörður by the name of Halla. Not much is known about her beginnings, in fact they have always been somewhat shrouded in mystery. Some say Halla was the sister of a well-known lady of deep knowledge, Elín, the witch of Elínarhöfði. It was whispered that the sisters had gained their knowledge by attending a school that taught more than the average one, but was extremely difficult to locate. Some say it is in the middle of the Black Forest in what is now Germany, while others claim that it is in Lapland, where all the most powerful magic in the world stems from. It was believed that in order to gain access to the school the pupils had to choose between themselves one to stay behind each year and serve the master of the school for eternity. The two sisters were not the only ones famous for attending that school, for so had also Sæmundur the wise, long before them, but that is a different story altogether. No one knows anything about this school for certain and should you like to attend it you will have to do your own research. What we do know is that Halla lived in Straumfjörður and was both wealthy and wise. She was much respected in the area and was known for her generosity and kindness, but she could be as hard as the skerries themselves if she got angry or felt she was being mistreated.

Halla had many people working on her farm, both family and workers. She had people fishing and she had people farming, and her farm was both a big one and a prosperous one. As was the custom of the time, the produce of the farm was delivered to the nearest merchant, who in return sold Halla items and food imported and not available by other means. The closest one to her at the time was some two days ride away, in Snæfellsnes, and he was a cheap and petty fellow. A poor farmer and a good friend of Halla had recently brought the merchant some very fine products, such as top-quality wadmal, thick and warm fabric woven from the wool of his sheep. The merchant had taken all of the excellent fabric and then made up a big debt that the farmer was supposed to be in, which was far from the truth. The poor man had to ride home with nothing and came to Halla in his despair to plead to her those wrong doings. 'It seems we will need to teach him a lesson,' she said, 'but for now I can help you out with what you need. If you want to help me in return, you can join my workers who are about to start swinging the scythes. When you are done here, I will send two men with you to help gather your own hay.'

The incredibly lush hay fields on the island and in the wetlands on shore were thick and tall and ready to be cut and dried. Her friend happily agreed to the deal, as it was a very generous offer indeed. He paired with four other and they prepared to leave to begin the cutting. 'Now, listen to me gentlemen,' spoke Halla before handing them each a scythe, two tents and provisions.

'You are to cut down the whole ness out by Greystone. You are to cut from morning till night and be done in four days' time. Each night, as you stop cutting, you are to place the scythes on the stone and head for your tents and your scythes will await you sharpened in the morning. None of you is to look at the scythes before dawn, nor into the edge of the blade or you will have to deal with me!' With that she sent them off to work.

When the men started cutting they were astonished over how sharp the scythes were. They sliced the thickest sedge like the blade was glowing and the sedge made of butter. They stayed that way from the first cut of the morning till the last stroke of the evening and the men made sure to do what Halla had ordered. That is, until the youngest in the pack had had enough. His curiosity burned and gnawed him all day long, and on the morning of the third day, as he was picking up his scythe, he looked into the edge of it. He let out a yelp of disgust and fright as he realised that the blade of his scythe was a man's rib, loosely tied to the wooden shaft. Immediately, the other scythes lost their form and revealed the ribs and it became clear that not much cutting would be done with these strange tools.

That same day Halla had been pondering her friend's troubles with the merchant. It was a foul thing he had done and not for the first time either. He had even cheated Halla herself and talked down her quality products every time she brought him her goods to sell. She, however, had an idea on to how to bring that man to his senses. She decided to consult with her sister, Ásta, who was wise and sharp as the scythes in her men's hands. Halla had a special place on the highest point of the cliff that faced the open waters outside her house. Whenever she needed her sister's advice or simply wanted to chat with her, she sat herself down on the edge of the cliff and said softly 'can you talk, sister dear?' Her sister had a place not unlike Halla's on her farm and would reply immediately, were she not too busy. The two sisters could thus enjoy a conversation across the bay of Faxaflói, and often did, even though it was a two-day crossing on a ship with full sails. Ásta replied that day and they spoke for a long time. They were good friends and Halla always felt like a load had been lifted off her shoulders whenever the two of them had enjoyed a conversation. They agreed on the merchant being taken down a peg as well as Ásta joining her sister to gather the hay being cut. They could feel approaching rain in their joints. They said their goodbyes with love, both looking forward to their meet.

When Halla was just about to head back home she saw one of her workers returning from the ness. 'Finished already are you? What mighty reapers I have in my service, to finish a four-day cutting in only two?'

The young man looked at the toes of his leather shoes, with his hands clutched together. 'I know what you did and what you saw, you fool. Go to the smithy and fetch five scythes little man. Do not forget the sharping stone as these are a bit more conventional and you need to do your own sharpening from here on.'

The young man muttered something underneath his breath and turned to the smithy. He did not return to his fellow workers until nightfall and they began the cutting bright and early the next day. The scythes were of good quality and bit fairly well, but needed constant sharpening and bit nothing close to the ones they had before. However, they were strong fellows and used to the job at hand so they finished in two days' time and returned home.

By the time they returned, Ásta's ship had just landed. The two sisters greeted each other lovingly as they had not met for a long time. The men were restless, as clouds of rain were beginning to approach land and they knew it would rain all too soon. They wanted to begin the tying and gathering as it would take days to transport all that hay on horses. They all met by the well the men had chopped and dug the previous summer and enjoyed the cold and crisp water from the bucket. 'Do not worry about that hay, us sisters are taking care of those few straws.'

'Few straws!' the men said and felt somewhat indignant. 'It took us days to cut that and it is going to rain into the ground if we do not start hauling it home right away,' said the oldest of her men.

Halla looked at him with fire in her eye. 'Remember your place, my good man. Step inside, all of you and eat whatever you fancy from the pantry. Drink ale and rest but do not dare to come out of the house until I let you.'

She turned to her sister. 'Shall we?' and the two of them headed for the hay pit.

The men reluctantly went inside but soon found happiness in the pantry, and in the massive barrel of ale Ásta had brought on her ship. They ate and they drank and did so happily, all but the young man who had looked in the edge of his scythe. He was restless and felt the others to be stupid and docile. He ate little and he ate fast and then went out the door to have a look at what was going on outside. He was shocked and afraid to discover that the door was as if nailed shut and could not be budged. He tried looking around it but saw nothing until he noticed a crack in the wood itself. He bowed down and peered out of the crack with one eye and immediately found himself stuck to the door with his arse sticking out into the tunnel, the hallway into the house, much to his fellow workers' amusement. 'That is what you get for not trusting Halla!' and they roared with laughter as they searched for the bottom of the barrel.

What the young man saw was, however, quite a sight. He could make out Ásta, standing in the big pit with the stone walls where the hay was traditionally gathered and kept for winter. Halla was nowhere in sight, but the biggest bales of hay he had ever seen now began to appear as if being blown by the wind on the horizon. They landed one by one in the pit, carefully guided by Ásta until the pit was more than full; in fact the stack of hay reached far above the highest row of stones, such was the amount of hay. Halla herself came riding the last bale like a horse. She opened the door of the farmhouse and said, 'Your curiosity and devotion is admirable, young man. I like your determination my friend.' With that he was free and she put him and the rest of her men to work cutting turf to cover the stack of hey. As the last strip of turf was placed on the heap, it started raining. As soon as the rain cleared some days later, Halla sent two men to her friend, as she had promised, to gather his hay for the winter.

The sisters enjoyed each other's company for a few days until it was time for Ásta to head home. Halla turned to her young worker once more. 'You and I are going to ride to Snæfellsnes to deposit some well-chosen goods with the dear merchant. Prepare six horses for the trip and make sure they are ready in two days. Fasten new horseshoes and make sure the carriers are unbroken and in good condition as their burdens will be heavy.'

The young man did as his mistress ordered, keen on not receiving more unusual punishments and to make up for his mistake earlier. When all was ready, he informed Halla. 'Go and pack your own things and meet me here when you are ready to travel,' she said, and took the reins of all six horses. She tied each to the next one's tail and when the young man came back with his gear each of the six horses was standing under bursting packs. Behind them stood twelve wethers (castrated rams), gloriously fat and covered with thick wool from head to tail.

'Off we go,' said Halla and led the way with the horses and the wethers following in a straight line as if under a spell.

Halla had two sons, and it so happened that they passed the farm of her eldest one. They arrived there around nightfall and Halla was ever so glad to see her son. 'Mother dear,' he said with a grin, as she got off her horse, 'unusually hard are the packs you carry to the merchant this time!'

'Shut up boy, it seems I have taught you a bit too much!'

They spent the night in good company and set off early the next day. They reached the merchant at midday and untied the packs and carried them in the storehouse. Big loads of butter, lard and wadmal was unpacked under the merchant's nose and not even that old ram could refuse that, the quality of it all was superb. Halla returned home that very same day with Brennivín and coffee, meal and sugar, leather and ale and many other sorts. When a short while had passed the merchant sent his errand boy to stack what Halla had brought and get it on the ship. The boy was shocked, to say the least, when he found nothing but a pile of rocks in the storehouse and twelve mice huddled in the pen where they had left the goods. 'That treacherous hag!' screamed the merchant, 'get in the saddles boys, we are going to bring her to justice or to her death!' They rode off with the merchant leading himself, angry as a wasp in a mug.

As soon as Halla noticed they were being followed she smiled and said to her companion, 'Little did he like the mice of Straumfjörður,' and as soon as she let the words go, they were covered in the thickest fog the young man had ever seen. He could hardly make out the horse in front of him and felt uneasy.

'Do not worry lad, the horses know the way and the merchant will learn his lesson. He would rather lay down and die than admit to being tricked by a woman,' said Halla, and had trouble hiding her giggles.

And she was very right. The merchant soon turned around with his tail between his legs. He made his men swear not to mention any of this to a living soul for the rest of their lives. He was less than happy whenever Halla appeared at his store from thereon, but at least he was a little fairer towards those dependent on his handling. As for Halla and her worker, they came home to Straumfjörður with everything ready for winter. The pantry was filled to the roof with what they had brought home as well as the abundance of food already smoked, dried, pickled and salted. The following spring Halla and her young worker were married, and it was said she had spent the winter teaching him a thing or two about the world not all of us get to see and live. She lived for many more years and when she passed away she was buried in a mound, just a stone's throw away from her house. There she still rests to this day and the mound is called Hölludys, or Halla's mound. Several place names in Straumfjörður bear witness to the time when she lived, even the well she had chopped in the bedrock is still there and the water just as fresh. I will let you guess the name of the well.

The Troll-wife
and the Reverend

Years and years ago, in fact all the way back to the dark time, there was a small church in the east of Iceland. It stood in the fjord Mjóifjörður and was a humble church, but a good one. In fact, it stills stands, and still has the same sky-piercing, jagged mountaintops watching over it and the same fog covering it when the sun sets. Perhaps it even has some of the same inhabitants peering at it with a mean frown through an opening in the mountain cliffs no human has ever stumbled upon. The fjord is narrow and pierces the eastern mountains, almost like a great iron ship steered by a giant, drunk out of his wits, and rammed against the cliffs in the times of Óðinn himself. Mjóifjörður is a beautiful place indeed; the weather there is unusually good, thanks to the shelter from the mountains, and the hills grow green and lush. It is therefore well suited for farming and people have been living well there for a very long time. With one exception though.

In a time when trolls roamed the highlands, one of

them, a particularly fierce troll-wife, made her dwellings in a cave in one of the canyons that splits up the mountains of Mjóifjörður. She was, as trolls tend to be in Iceland, enormous, strong as a berserker and with a temper like the howling wind in the midst of a snowstorm. She ate whatever she could get her hands on: horses, sheep, reindeer, sharks and, of course, people. Over the years, and they were counted in the hundreds, she had developed a sweet tooth. Her absolute favourite was a young priest, as they tasted, for some reason, sweeter and were quite a lot tenderer than a worn-out farmer or an overworked seaman. She was therefore quite happy with her cave, as it was only a few strides away from the church. New priests kept turning up and she lured them into her arms. During a priest's first service in the church she would make her way through the graveyard and pass her grey, hairy paw, by the window and make sure the priest saw it. This would drive the priest instantly insane and he would shout over the churchgoers; 'Tear away my guts and my innards, my liver and my lungs, I am headed for the canyon!' With that he would rip off his hemp and, with a crazed look on his face, run out of the church never to be seen again.

Understandably, this led to some difficulty when it came to finding priests to service the church in Mjóifjörður, as word spread among them. Keeping a pest of this magnitude secret proved difficult, even for the bishop of Iceland. Eventually no one would take the job, the troll-wife went back to eating whatever she could find and the farm, along with the church, fell into ruin. Years passed, houses collapsed, people moved away (or got eaten) and finally only a handful of people struggled in the fjord. A young man by the name of Valtýr was around that time finishing his studies and becoming a priest. Valtýr had grown up with his grandmother, a wise old woman who knew further than her nose reached, as we say, and had taught her grandson a thing or two no one can learn in an ordinary school. Valtýr began his search for a flock and a church, but found nothing. Every position was already filled, every church had its priest and new openings fell to the sons of priests. After a while though, he did come across a place, a fjord in the east plagued by a dark shadow that no one would even talk about, except in whispers. Valtýr, however, brave as he was and wise, took on the church in Mjóifjörður despite many warnings from his fellow clergymen. He travelled with his few belongings across the whole land and arrived at his new home in spring, as the ground was peering from under the snow and rivers beginning to break their bonds of ice. He was met with a bleak sight, a farm that once stood proud and a church that had lost its glory.

With a steady hand and a firm mind, Valtýr began to rebuild the farm and gather the few farm animals left in the fjord. He built walls and thatched roofs, milked sheep and cows and remarkably soon he had changed the derelict ruins into a prosperous farm once more and people flocked around the young priest. Work started on the old church, and in a matter of weeks it too stood rebuilt and freshly painted. Other farms in the community attracted people once more and the whole land began to rise once more.

One day, Valtýr took some time from his hard work to look around the area. He found himself riding his horse up a deep, narrow canyon when he came across an opening, a cleft, indeed, it was a cave. He dismounted the horse and peered into the darkness of the cave. As his eyes adjusted to the darkness he could make out the outlines of a huge figure, crouched over something between her hands. Finally, the young man was face to face with the troll that had taken so many lives and caused so much devastation. As the troll-wife stretched her back, she sniffed into the darkness and spoke in a voice as course as a rockslide on a mountainside; 'Well, if it isn't the new priest, my next sweet meal.'

Startled, Valtýr thought hard of his next move and to buy him some time he asked the troll what she was clutching between her crooked paws. 'Oh my dear, this is just the skull of Reverend Flóki. I am gnawing away the rest of his hardened flesh and am growing hungry for more.' This was too much even for our brave young priest and he ran as fast as his feet would carry him out into the light, jumped on his horse and rode away in much haste. The bellowing laughter of the troll-wife followed him as he rode out of the canyon, loosening boulders and mud, which fell dangerously close to his way to safety.

Valtýr thought long and hard as the days passed. It was now time for his first service in the lovely church and he, along with his growing flock, was both looking forward to the day and dreading it. Eventually the day dawned, as they tend to. He summoned twelve men to him that morning, twelve strong men who he trusted and knew to have a cool head and a steady hand. 'As soon as you notice me losing my mind,' he told his men, 'I want six of you to jump on me and hold me pinned to the church floor, and I want six of you to charge up the church tower and fiercely ring both bells to the point of cracking!' The men agreed reluctantly; they had grown quite fond of their young priest and would rather have him uneaten for the time being. Indeed, some of the people had suggested that the priest should not hold a service at all, but he would not hear of it.

As Valtýr began his sermon over his friends and neighbours, the inevitable happened. The horrid paw flickered against the window, and Valtýr lost his marbles. 'Tear away my guts and my innards, my liver and my lungs, I am headed for the canyon!' he shouted from the top of his voice, with a mad look in his eyes.

His trusted twelve did, however, not fail him. Six of the biggest ones jumped on the priest and struggled to hold him down as he fought them with a might no one had ever witnessed before. Clothes were torn, wood was splintered and curses fouler than a rancid pit ran from the mad priest. The other six, meanwhile, rushed up the tower and took turns in ringing the church bells, on and on with all their strength. The noise inside the church was unbearable and the people ran for what they feared was their life. What they saw standing in the graveyard made them stand as still as stones, and their blood froze. A troll, angry as a ram in battle and as big as their church tower, stood with her paws covering her ears, screaming in pain, so loud that she drowned the thundering bells. With a look that could kill a horse, and in fact did kill one of the horses in the pen behind the church, she gazed over the people, grinding her teeth, swaying back and forth like a tree in a storm. Overpowered by the ringing bells and defeated, she sprang away from the noise, jumping in one stride all the way to the graveyard wall and stepped on the top of the wall. As she pushed herself away from the wall, many of the well-laid stones forming it rolled down from their seats and left an opening, almost as big as the gate itself. Turning her head with the same horrid look in her eyes she shouted, 'Never stand!' She ran off screaming into the mountains, never to be seen again to this day.

Valtýr took a long time to recover from the ordeal, but he did. He became a respected and just member of his community and served his flock until he died a very old man. He never spoke of that day or the troll-wife, not until on his deathbed, when he told his young apprentice what to do if the troll ever showed its face again. And now you know as well.

When you find yourself in Iceland, Mjóifjörður should be one of your destinations. When you visit the church, make sure you take a look at the stone wall by the old graves there. The gap in the stonework is still there and can, to this day, not be mended, as the stones will never stand.

The Demon
on the Beam

ólar in Hjaltadalur valley is the name
of a long-established church. In fact,
it is where the bishop of north Iceland
resided and was, at the time of our story
(and still is), a bustling village. It served
as the capital of the north for 700 years,
wealthy and high raised, the home of one of the country's universities for centuries. The surrounding area is a
beautiful one, the mountain Hólabyrða lends shelter, tall
and mighty, and thick grass grows in the shelter on the
flatlands around the village.

One of the bishops, one of the first ones in Christianity
back in the time we know little of, was a man of great
knowledge. His knowing extended even in to the world
of magic and his flock treaded carefully with him around.
The church farm, or village, was a bustling one with
many maids and workers doing various jobs. The blacksmith worked the bellows and the hammer on the anvil
in the big smithy all day long and the weaver worked the
loom just as hard. Young and strong women milked the

many cows and churned the butter, with sweat on their brows, and able men built houses for the bishop as well as labouring in the fields. Each person had a job and knew their job, and Þorkell, the young man responsible for the feeding and the care of the many cows on the estate, was no different. Well, maybe he was a bit different. He was a strapping young lad, hard working and good looking, intelligent and witty, but he had a foul mouth and an even worse temper. He knew every swear word in the language and he knew a few he had made up himself. Every time he was spoken to he would snort back with a harsh tongue and never had anything nice to say. Needless to say, he was not a very popular man and people avoided him and his temper. Whenever things did not go his way he would erupt like a volcano, breaking and throwing things in a fit of anger with the profanities spewing from his mouth like wet dung spread from a shovel.

The people around him grew tired of this and one of them was chosen to speak to the head man. He spoke to Þorkell, who, with a grin on his face, promised to better himself, but did not do so in any way. Again, the head man tried to get him to behave, but he did not change his ways in the slightest. One morning, the head man and one of the maids were talking behind a stack of peat when the bishop himself was walking by. Normally he did not bother with such small matters as a foul-mouthed worker, but the conversation caught his attention and he listened. 'I will tell you,' said the head man to the maid, 'he is on his last chance. There are plenty of willing people that would want his job and even though he does it well, this is no way to behave.'

The bishop decided to take this matter into his own hands. The next day he had Þorkell called into his study.

'I hear you have a foul mouth young man, and a temper to go with it. I will not tolerate that, but I will give you your final chance of keeping your job. I have arranged for someone to keep an eye on you and when you enter the cow shed you will notice you have company.'

Þorkell dared not utter a word, he bowed and backed out of the study. 'Who does he think he is,' he muttered to himself, 'telling me what to say and not to say, that old git, that foul blister of a man, that retched old ram.'

From there the words got even dimmer, until he reached the cow shed. He opened the door, like so many times before, and expected to see some old lady from the village, or maybe a child sent there to listen to his every word, but he could not see a living soul.

'Ugly old bag of a bishop,' he loudly yelled at one of the cows after he had firmly closed the door and immediately he heard a snicker from above. He looked up into the thick cobwebs swaying in the shadows of the roof beams and gasped. There, on one of the strong collar beams, there sat a greyish little thing with a thin tail and an ugly face. The tail swung lazily like the tail of a cat too full to move and with a mouse in its sights, and its eyes glowed like burning coals. It burped and grinned as Þorkell looked down and remembered the words of the bishop.

The days passed and Þorkell paid no attention to the critter on the beam, in fact he made an effort not to look at it as it burped and snickered at his every word. One afternoon he did look up though, after a long string of profanity from him towards a very pretty milkmaid, who he secretly adored, and an unusually loud burp from the critter. Much to his dismay he now saw a fully formed demon perched on the same beam. Not only had it turned jet black, but was now as fat as a barrel. Its sides and belly wriggled like beestings milk pudding and its cheeks drooped down like snow from a pine branch. The milkmaid screamed at the top of her voice and ran out, slamming the door behind her. The thing looked at him with anticipation in its glowing eyes, and Þorkell felt the anger swelling up inside him. For the first time he spoke to the demon. 'You rancid pile of filth, what are you doing here, you disgusting bag of droppings?'

To his dismay, he saw the demon chew eagerly on the mouthful he had given him, with a grin, growing even wider. 'My dear Þorkell, I thought you would never ask! I am the demon on the beam, sent here by my master as a favour to your master, to sit here and eat your every bad word, every outburst toward the milkmaids, every bad gesture, every frown and every punch and kick you give the cows. When I have had my fill, and you are, I must say, providing me very well, I will drag you with me to where I belong and where you will serve my master to the end of time.'

Þorkell felt his stomach plummet and his heart sink. His breathing got heavier as fear crept up his spine and took hold. For the first time in his life he feared for himself, a crack in his arrogance let in doubt and worries. He took back to his work, feeding the cows in silence and vowed that he would not spend eternity wherever that demon came from.

Over the next few days Þorkell made an effort not to swear, nor to even throw a glance at the demon. He kept quiet and kept to himself and did his job with the utmost most attention to detail and the well-being of the animals. When Halla, the milkmaid he was beginning to like more with every passing day, came in to milk the cows he smiled at her and felt his heart beat just a little faster with each time they met. He even found himself in conversation one morning with two of the other workers, as they talked amongst themselves about going ice skating on the river soon.

With every day that passed he felt more relieved, and had even taken to softly singing some of the songs his grandmother had sung for him before she passed away and things took a turn for the worse in his life. One morning, after a wonderful conversation with his new friend Halla, he could not help but cast a quick glance at the demon and was not met with a pretty sight. It had shrunk back even thinner than it had first been, and was now sitting on the beam wrinkled, withered and grey like an old, dry leather pouch. The eyes were hardly a glimmer in the dark any more, its tail was but a string and its teeth, which had been like big white pearls, were now black and rotting away. 'Oh, so you do remember me,' the demon crowed, 'I am wasting away because of you, Þorkell, hunger gnaws me from within and I am going mad up here, please feed me, feed me like before!' But Þorkell simply looked away and shrugged.

When he left his cottage to work the next morning the sun was shining and he looked around, hoping to see Halla. He greeted a few of the people in the village, who by now greeted him back, leaving a smile on his face and a feeling of lightness in his chest. He found his way, as so often before, to the bishop's cow shed, but knew from afar that something was terribly wrong. Inside, he was met with utter chaos. All the cows were tied together by their tails, screaming and roaring in anger, fright and pain. Every pen, shelf, barrel and table was broken to dust and in the middle of all this stood what was left of the demon, with a horrid, twisted smile on its skinny face. Þorkell grabbed a broken shovel from the debris and swung at the demon, blinded by anger and hate. He ran around the shed for a good while, tying together the most awful curses he had ever heard, screaming, yelling, swinging at the demon again and again and driving the cows even closer to madness with his fit of rage. He finally came too, exhausted, crying and broken, lying in a heap of rubble that was once the interior of his fine cow shed. He looked around, and then up, and saw the demon glaring at him from the beam, black as the night and fatter than ever.

Þorkell got to his feet and remembered his vows and his newfound friends. Without so much as one word he took to calming the cows and untying them, one tail at a time. He then fed them and calmed them as well as he could and began to repair the inside of the shed in silence. He remembered one of his grandmother's songs and calmed his soul by softly singing to himself and the cows and spent the whole night working by the light of a single candle. When the sun rose he had repaired most of the damage and led each cow back to its stall with a whisk of good hay and fresh water. His spirits were up, and he decided to go and look for Halla. He found her on her way to do the morning milking, with her pretty smile and her rosy cheeks, and he stopped her in her path. He smiled and took her hands in his and they shared their first kiss of many.

Over the next weeks the cows of the bishop of Hólar gained a reputation for giving the most milk and the best. The butter of the estate glowed with fat, the cream was as thick as if it had been frozen and the skyr (yoghurt) was so tart, people had never tasted anything like it. The bishop himself came to see Þorkell in the cow shed and see for himself how well the cows were being looked after and how clean and happy they were. Indeed, Þorkell was now as happy as his cows, with his love and Halla's growing every day, and them talking between themselves about maybe getting married one day. In fact, they did so that very summer, and who better to hitch them together than the bishop himself.

Halla and Þorkell made a good life for themselves and their handful of little ones that came later, born in the house their parents built for them and for their life together. Luck and joy followed the family more so than wealth, but the children grew up to get a good education in the university and became good people, every last one. The only one not happy at all was the demon on the beam, who soon dropped dead into the dung below.

The Skeleton

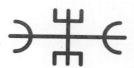

Þuríður was a woman who did not call everything her grandmother. And why, you might rightfully ask, should anyone call anything grandmother except his or her grandmother? Well, I am afraid I have no answer to that. It is one of the very quirky sayings that we have over here on our odd island. When we describe someone who is afraid of nothing or no one, this is a very good way to do just that. And that is exactly the way to describe Þuríður. She was a grown woman when our story takes place and had seen a thing or two unfold in her life. She had been at sea and she had worked on land, she had known love and she had known loss, she had experienced hardship and she had known joy. Her hard work and quick wit had got her a very good position for someone of her status, being the daughter of poor farmers. She was now a head maid and a key holder in a rectory, working for a widowed priest as old as a troll-man.

The old church had its relics and oddities, as often is the case in old churches, but this one had an oddity to say the least. The skeleton of a man, old and yellow and hanging together by strains of dried-out flesh and sinews,

lay under the aft-most bench and had done so for as long
as the eldest men remembered. No one knew to whom it
had belonged, nor why it was there, but many attempts
had been made to bury it, to no avail. It had been placed
on top of caskets, underneath them, besides them and
even in them. A special burial had been tried for the
bones but every single time, the morning after the burial,
it would be found lying on top of the ground with not
a scrap of mud or soil on it and the freshly closed grave
unspoiled. It was a known secret that the old priest had
even taken it far into the heath when his people from the
farm went to collect mountain grass to eke out the bread
meal through the winter. There he left it, between two
rocks for the elements to take care of, but, it was once
more in the church the day after, long before he and the
people came home from their picking. The only place
it seemed to lay in peace was under that bench, but it
emitted coldness and hostility from under there and no
one liked to sit on the aft-most bench.

One dark and frosty evening the priest was getting
ready to read to his household from the saltere or
the Graduale, which were books of outtakes from
the Bible. This was a very common practice while the
people of Iceland were still ruled by the church as much
as the authorities and was usually done by the man of
the house, or whoever could read in the house. If such
a person was to be found, that is. He then remembered
he had left the saltere in the church and asked Þuríður
if she could go and fetch it. 'Of course I can,' she said,
and turned around. 'You do not fear the skeleton then,
in the dark church? You are a fearless woman, Þuríður,
and I bet I could have asked you to bring in the skeleton itself.'

She smiled and winked at the old man before storming out of the house and to the church. When she came back the pair of them shared a laugh as she had not only brought the saltere, but the skeleton as well, holding it like a baby on her hip. 'I am not sure we are paying our full respect my dear,' said the priest as he stroked away a tear of laughter, 'but I think this one is used to all sorts of treatments by now.' The two of them laughed some more before Þuríður brought the skeleton back to the church.

Much to her surprise, she saw on her way over that the candles in the church were now lit, even though she had not lit a single candle before. Even more to her surprise, the skeleton, which had until now remained as quiet as you might expect from a skeleton, began to speak. Its jaw rattled loose and its teeth clattered so it was not easy to make out the words, but it was a calm night and Þuríður could make out the words.

'When you enter the church, it will be filled with people. They will all be quiet, and you need not utter a word to any of them except for one man, sitting on the front-most bench. He will be clad in red and have a red hat on, and I ask you to do me one service. He is the reason why I cannot rest in peace, as I did him a great wrong, many moons ago, and he cursed me to never get my rest. See if you can soften him up and persuade him to lift the curse, as it binds both of us and neither one can be at peace until he does. I have suffered enough and so has he and he must see that and understand. Do this, and I will make sure your fortune will be great from now on.'

Just as the skeleton had predicted, the church was full of people when she entered. She paid no attention to them, although she recognised one or two that she knew to be very dead.

She lay down the skeleton in an empty seat in the back and found the man in red. 'Is it not time that you forgive and forget, and with that find your own peace?' she asked. 'Haven't both of you suffered enough, whatever it was that happened between you and binds you two together with such great force?'

'No,' the man in red replied, 'it will never be time.'

'In that case, I will raise a few ghosts up myself,' Þuríður said to the gloomy figure, 'and see to it that they spend eternity haunting you and pestering you in every way possible. I will see to it that you will not have a moment's peace for as long as you hold on to your grudge against that poor pile of bones over there.'

She looked at the skeleton sitting between two well-clad but frowning ladies, who were obviously not too happy with their new friend. At this time deep mumblings of approval were heard from the people. 'Has it not been long enough, man?'

'It is time this nonsense ended.'

'His crime was not that great to begin with if you ask me.'

It seemed that the whole congregation agreed and the man in red finally gave in. 'Very well, perhaps it is time we rested,' he said reluctantly, looking at the skeleton. 'But I will never forget what you did.'

'Fine by me,' said the skeleton, this time dropping its jaw all the way down on to the collarbone, but swiftly putting it back in place. 'I have all but turned to dust and am more than tired of laying under this dusty bench.'

'Leave then, in peace, every one of you!' shouted the man in red and they all vanished before Þuríður's eyes, except the man in red and the skeleton. She could have sworn that it gave her both a little nod and a smile, although she was never sure how the thing managed the smile when she later thought of that strange evening.

Þuríður turned her back to the man in red and could not help but feel a little sorry for him, as he sat there all alone with his head hanging down. As she was reaching for the door, he spoke to her again. 'Look, look, look into my black eye, once before you leave Þuríður.'

Despite not calling everything her grandmother, this sent chills down her spine and froze the blood in her veins. 'What an evil man this one must have been,' she thought to herself, 'the bugger wants to drag me into the grave with him, if I am not mistaken!'

Out loud she said, 'Look, look, look into my black arse, you foul git,' as she pulled up the backside of her skirt all the way up to her back, and leaned over for a second. She then left the church and went inside, where she acted as if nothing had happened out of the ordinary.

A few weeks later a burial was to take place in the cemetery. Þuríður asked the old priest to try one more time to bury the poor thing laying under the benches, but he saw no use in repeating what had been tried so many times before. 'This time it might be different, and I strongly urge you to try once more.'

He gave in, knowing that Þuríður had lived her share of years and that it is usually best to heed the advice of women. The skeleton was buried that day, along with an old farmer, and their grave was filled as tradition has it. The next morning, much to everyone's surprise not a single bone was found under the benches. No one ever saw the man in red after that, and still has not to this very day.

Þuríður soon married after these strange events, to a young and handsome man who worshipped the very ground she walked on. She lived for a long time in good health and much wealth, and that is all I know of her to tell.

Seven on Land,
Seven in Sea

Ýrdalur is on the south coast of Iceland. Beaches of black sand and boulders stretch as far as the eye can see, and the waves of the ocean mercilessly pound it, but sometimes they stroke the land, in a rhythm as old as the mountains and the glaciers that line the coast. Deserts of the blackest sand cover land as big as counties and hold within their wet grasps the wrecks of hundreds and hundreds of stranded ships, and all the goods that people could not save, as well as all the lives that no one could reach. The shoreline keeps changing, moving further out with every grain of sand the glacial rivers carry from the highland, thus keeping the land alive and the shipwrecks hidden.

In the village of Vík, a long time ago, there lived a fisherman named Eyvindur. He was a handsome one, strong as an ox and built like one, with blue eyes that saw far and his beard was as dark as the beaches he knew so well. He was a fisherman and set out in his boat, rowed by eight men, every day the gods of the sea and wind would allow him, to fetch the silver from the sea. He was a good captain with a good boat. It had been built by his father, who could make each board of the boats he built follow his will as if it could hear him and understand. His father had passed away by the time of our story, but Eyvindur still lived with his mother, who was old and weak, but he thought the world of her and took the best care of her that he possibly could. Their house was just above the naust, where his boat sat in shelter when not at sea, and the turf-covered camp where his crew lived for a good part of each year.

Even though he was a grown man, and a proud one as well, he listened to his mother's every word and had long since learned to heed her advice when it came to weather and wind. If she would stick out her nose into a gentle breeze and blue skies and said, 'Do not sail,' he would not go, and the weather would turn that day and lives would be lost. If she stuck the same nose out in a blizzard and said, 'Row boy, when the snowfall clears up a bit,' he would prepare his boat and crew and be off at the first glimpse of blue sky through the snow, those days beating all the other boats to the best fishing grounds. He did as his mother suggested, in most matters, but not those of the heart.

Eyvindur had been of age for a while now and the old woman wanted to see her grandchildren before she said her goodbyes to this world. Every now and then she would suggest one of the fine ladies in Vík, or a farmer's daughter in the area, but each time Eyvindur would smile inside his bushy beard and give his mother a kiss on the cheek. 'I will know when I meet her mother,' he would say, and she would reply, 'And I'll be stone cold when you do boy!' Somehow he knew that there was a woman waiting for him, just as he was waiting for her.

One summer evening in the glowing midnight sun, Eyvindur went for a stroll along the beach, thinking that he would perhaps wind up at a friend's house. His boat was in the naust after a good day of fishing and his crew sat around a fire in front of their camp with a bottle of Brennivín. He passed a tall cliff he had climbed every day as a child and was met with a strange sight. There, in front of him, on the jet black sand, lay several skins. He picked one of them up and saw it for a seal-skin, soft and beautiful, and he could sense the faintest aroma of the flowers of the summer from it. He then heard voices. He heard people singing and laughing, and with great caution, he approached a cave, just a few strides away. He hid himself behind a big boulder and looked inside. His heart skipped a beat as he looked at a group of the most beautiful women he had ever seen, dancing, singing and laughing in the sand, as naked as he had been himself on the day he was born. He looked away, ashamed for looking, but still so eager to see, he clutched the skin between his hands and smelled it with a smile on his face as he listened to the magic of the song of the selkies inside the cave.

Finally, the singing stopped and he peered from his hideout once more. He could see the selkies putting on their skin and disappearing into the foaming sea one by one, except for the one most beautiful of them all. She looked and she looked in terror, behind stones and in clefts, in the water and on the sand. When she was alone on the beach with a grave expression and a tear in her eye, Eyvindur took a step from behind the boulder and showed himself. She looked at him with the deepest, darkest eyes he had ever seen and they bound his soul. 'Eyvindur, have you taken my skin? What would you need with the skin of a selkie? You have caught plenty of seals in your time and have many skins.'

He just stood there, lost for words at the proud, beautiful creature in front of him. 'How would you know,' he said astounded, 'and how do you know my name? What is your name?'

'We know much about man folk, and I know much about you, Eyvindur. My name is Indíana.' She approached him, with her eyes fixed on his and kissed him a deep kiss. 'I have waited for a long time to meet you Eyvindur and you have been waiting for me. Now that I have, I might not be going in the sea for a while, if you will have my company. Make sure to keep that skin safe for me and where it won't tempt me.'

She kissed him again and again and he felt as if he floated on air as they walked to his home.

Eyvindur locked the skin in a chest in his smithy, as soon as the two of them came home, and put the key around his neck. Indíana, having put on some of Eyvindur's clothes, looked around curiously as she studied the life of the land folk, and met the old lady. The pair of them became friends in an instant and Eyvindur could simply not believe his fortune. As this wonderful day came to an end, Indíana noticed the key around Eyvindur's neck. 'Keep it there my dear, and keep it safe,' she said as she began to drown him in the sweetest kisses he could have ever imagined.

The years passed and the old lady got her wish. Before she said her goodbyes she had met three of her grandchildren, a boy and two girls, all of them healthy as a horse in summer. After her passing, the family grew

⊙⟩‖⟩⟩⟨⊙

and grew, four, five, six, seven children the couple had
between them, after many happy years together. Indíana
was very fond of her dark man, as she lovingly called him,
and Eyvindur could not see the stars for her beauty and
wit. She kept very much to herself and was considered
very mysterious and wise by their few friends and their
neighbours. She rarely spoke to anyone but Eyvindur
and her children and she told them stories of a land that
seemed as far away as the moon, yet felt so close they
could travel there in a heartbeat. In that land life was different, yet so strangely similar to their life together, and
she would always have upon her face the expression of
deepest sorrow when she told them her tales. She would
often walk the black beaches below the village, singing
in a low voice, and people whispered among themselves
about a herd of seals that would follow her, just off
shore, whichever way she walked along the beach.

With time, Indíana grew sadder and sadder and
Eyvindur felt her troubles, although she would not tell
him what was bothering her. Her stories got fewer and
further apart and her smile was less and less with each
day. Her walks on the beach grew longer and Eyvindur
knew full well what was bothering his soulmate. She
kept on showing her love for her family, and for her
dark man, but her troubles grew.

One morning, Eyvindur lay in bed and watched her
back as she got up, her hair black as the beaches flowing
down her back and her beauty once more took his
breath away. She turned around and smiled at him and
he smiled back, knowing that he was the luckiest man
alive. With her out of their small bedroom he took the
key he had around his neck and placed it gently on her
pillow. He then prepared for a day at sea, as he had done

so many, many times before, and was off with his crew with a tear in his eye.

As soon as Indíana entered their room to grab her own set of keys to the house, she saw what was lying on her pillow. She slowly picked up the key that both held her captive and gave her all her joy and laughter. She put the key around her neck and found her seven children. She cried as she kissed each and every one of them goodbye, and all she said to each one was, 'Hear my haunting plea, I have seven on land and seven in the sea.' She opened the smithy and unlocked the chest, and took out her sealskin, as pristine as the day she had taken it off to dance on the beach. Crying, she ran down to the shore and put on her skin for the last time. She took one look at her house and her children, who had followed her, and was gone with the waves.

Eyvindur knew what she had chosen before his boat even touched the sand. He was met by his seven children, the oldest holding the youngest, and all of them had the expression of someone with a broken heart. He took them home and comforted them by the fire burning in the hearth, as he explained to them how the heart has to have what it most wants, even if that breaks other hearts. He raised the children well and he raised them alone from then on. They shared the stories of their mother with each other and remembered her for her love and laughter for all their days. It was said that whenever one of them, or all of them, would come near to the sea, wherever they were, they would be met by eight seals, each one more beautiful than the last and the biggest one of them cried and called out in despair.

Perhaps when you tread the black beaches of south Iceland, or any beach for that matter, you will catch a glimpse of a seal, maybe even a herd of them. Should such luck find you, make sure to look one of them deeply in the eye as it curiously watches you, bobbing up and down gracefully on the waves close to shore. You just might be looking into the eyes of someone you will meet further on in life.

The Ghost's Cap

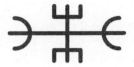

i n the small village of Eyrarbakki on the south coast of Iceland there once lived a young woman. She was born and raised in the village and worked as a maid in the doctor's house. She was both intelligent and diligent, and was liked by the people in the household as well as the whole village. Well, she was liked by almost all. In the same house there lived and worked an errand boy who did not like the young woman all that much. In fact, he did not seem to like anyone for that matter, his favourite pastime was to trick and startle people day in and day out, and frankly people were getting rather tired of the boy and his mischief. They had long since lost the count of how many times he had tripped the maids in the stairs, how many times he had startled the old kitchen lady, how many times he had splashed water on the cat or how many times he had hid in the doctor's office and eavesdropped on important conversations only to run to the store and blurt it all out. Everyone was getting tired of the boy and suspected he would be let go sooner than later.

The doctor's house was positioned in the heart of the village, next to the church along with the cemetery. The garden fence around the house acted as the cemetery wall on one side, with only a few steps from the house to the most outer graves. A nice, narrow gate was on the wooden fence, built on the doctor's orders, apparently to make it easier to drive the sheep away from his yard that sometimes wandered in there. Why they should rather graze in the cemetery no one knew, and it was probably only a coincidence that when the doctor and the priest had the urge to drink a little something heart-warming to each other's health, they could do so without the immediate danger of the good doctor tumbling over the fence in the thick of night on his way home from such meetings. Such a household as the doctor's meant a lot of washing of clothes, linen and gauzes. Because of that, a long clothesline had been strung between two logs found on the beach below the village, half buried with the thicker end down, as is the better way to go about such doing. Our young woman was no stranger to the clothesline as she made trip after trip out behind the house to hang and collect, between her toiling over the steaming washtub and the washboard in the washing room.

One dark and gloomy night, she was at last in her bed when she remembered she had left the doctor's collection of night caps, along with a few of his knitted long pants, dangling on the line out back. She cussed quickly and quietly before getting out of the warm bed and stepped on the freezing floor. She, of course, could not have the whole town seeing her employer's underpants waving like a flag when day broke. She wrapped a shawl around her shoulders and tiptoed down the steep stairs as to not wake up the other people, long since sleeping a worry-free sleep. She bowed her head as she left the house out the back door and ran over to the clothesline to start gathering the doctor's closest garments.

When she thought she had everything, something white caught her attention out of the corner of her eye. 'That little imbecile, that rascal, that little git,' she thought to herself as she hurried towards the little gate in the fence. There, sitting on a gravestone in the middle of the cemetery, she saw that little annoying errand boy with one of the doctor's caps on his head. She paced between the graves until she reached him and tore the cap from the boy's head in a rough manner. She then slapped him hard across the cheek, shouting 'You don't scare me you little fool, and you never will again. I'll see to it that you are kicked out of this house first thing in the morning!'

With that, she turned around with her nose in the air and stormed inside. She placed the pile of clothes neatly on a counter in the washroom and eagerly but quietly made her way to her awaiting bed.

She woke up in the grey beginnings of an autumn day and was soon dressed and in the washroom. Yawning and stretching, and with her eyes half closed, she sorted through what she had fetched the night before. Suddenly her heart skipped a beat and she was wide awake. The last of the white night caps was not so white, but covered in dirt and had holes in it. It was different from the others and somehow felt cold between her fingers as she remembered the incident in the cemetery the night before. With her heart racing and out of breath, she opened up a crack on the back door and stuck her head out. There, still sitting on the grave, was the same figure as from the night before, crouched over nothing and bare headed with its hands clutched together. She let out a small scream and slammed the door. She ran in the house and found the doctor and told him the whole story with tears streaming down her cheeks.

It so happened that the doctor was recovering after one of his meetings with the priest the night before. He somehow trusted his friend across the fence much better to deal with such a thing as a ghost on a gravestone, so he took the young lady to see the priest. On their way over, the two of them saw the being, still crouched the same way, clenching its hands together and not moving in any way. They woke up the priest and after a strong dose of the medicine from the night before he was as good as new. 'This fellow is obviously very upset,' said the priest. 'Did you offend him in any way?'

'I might have,' she replied, 'and I just might have something of his as well.'

'Give it back and he will find his way,' said the priest, now more worried about the room beginning to spin on its own than the troubles of a maid next door.

'Just do it in peace and do not anger that poor soul any more than you already have.'

As they got back the whole house was both curious and afraid of what sat in the cemetery. Most of the village was there by now and people lined the fence with their hearts thumping and their palms sweating as they stared at it in terror but could not look away. The young woman fetched the dirty cap from the washing room and slowly, step by step, crossed the back yard of the house and found herself once more treading between the graves. She stopped in front of the ghost and in silence placed the cap back on its head. The ghost did not even move a muscle, let alone express any form of gratitude for getting the cap back. As she backed away, a small voice inside her head said, 'Well, how ungrateful.' Aloud she said, 'Are you happy then?'

Quick as a kicking horse, the ghost slapped the girl across her face with such force to knock her to the ground. 'I am, but how about you,' it shrieked as it got up and vanished into the grave beneath the stone it had been sitting on. The young woman lay unconscious by the foot of the gravestone with a great red mark where the ghost had hit her. As the villagers returned home one by one, the doctor picked up his maid, and with a sense of affection that surprised him as well as frightened, he carried her inside the house.

She slept for days, and the doctor was all but beginning to think that she was lost, when she finally woke up. She had no memory of the ghost or the slapping, but bore the red mark on her cheek as a reminder of what can happen if you infuriate one who is in fact, very dead. She soon recovered and was back doing her duties as a maid in a short while. She could swear from then on that the good doctor kept eying her as she worked and even blushed when she brought him his evening coffee.

The young boy got his share of telling off and slapping about, but the doctor saw no reason to send him away. After all, that is what he was, a young boy, and the doctor encouraged him from there on to read and learn and to misbehave in a more fulfilling way than before. I have heard that the boy became a doctor himself one day, in that very house, but let us not believe everything we are told, or indeed, what we read.

Of Trolls

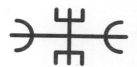

A troll is no laughing matter. Our neighbours in the east have their trolls as well, and they range from trowies on the islands to the big brutes on the mainland, and all of them are treacherous things, but none are like the trolls in Iceland. They are massive things, towering in height with the width and girth of a whale and strong as a pile of young oxen. One story tells of a troll-wife who wanted to wade from Norway to Iceland after she had visited a friend of hers. She was well aware of some very deep trenches on the bottom on her way, but was all but sure she would be tall enough to cross.

'Deep are the trenches round Iceland, though I am sure I can wade through them,' she said to her friend, and it became a saying. She got close to home, in fact she had almost made it all the way, when she tripped over a whale in one of those deep, deep trenches and fell over. As she fell, she reached for a ship that happened to be passing at the same time, but luck had abandoned her and she missed it by mere inches. She drowned, the poor thing and drifted ashore in Rauðisandur in the West Fjords some time later. She was so big, they say, that a fellow who happened to be riding there on a horse one day could not reach the hollow of her knee with his whip.

According to some tales, trolls are about as smart as a pile of oxen as well, but that cannot be. Not all of them at least, for then they would have died out a long time ago in the harsh surroundings they chose for themselves to live in. More stories describe how clever they are and, of course, they must be. A breed that has lived with the land for so long gains wisdom that is compared to no other. Should you want a little bit of that knowledge for yourself you need to make your way into the middle of Hallmundarhraun lava field in west Iceland on New Year's Eve. If you manage to hide well enough you will hear the troll-wives of the area as they compare their knowledge through the entire night. If they find you, they will eat you, and you need to stand the entire time on a twelve-winter-old vixen. Whether the vixen is then to be killed or set free afterwards is not entirely known, but I urge you to let it live.

If you have ever been in the highlands in the winter-time and experienced a snowstorm, or been badly lost in the thickest autumn fog up there, with every rock seeming like a tower in the grey, you get the feeling for a troll's temper. They are coarse and cold as the wind-swept, jagged mountain tops, and they usually want their privacy up there as well. If you climb a mountain as you go after a particularly stubborn ewe, you need to be prepared for all sorts of weather and all sorts of encounters, for you never know who or what you might startle. It is only when trolls develop a taste for human flesh that they prey upon men, yet some trolls develop a different kind of taste for people. Quite a few have found the shelter of a cave on such nights, as described before, only to be swept into a giant bed for a night or two. Indeed, some have even decided to turn their back on the world of men after such an experience. Two men were once sent deep into the heaths in west Iceland to collect mountain grass, a thick kind of moss that grows wild and was a part of the staple diet for centuries. One of them found himself high in the slopes of Réttarmúli when he saw a troll sitting on top of Eggjar, a black, jagged cliff that pierces the sky. She made a calm 'come hither' gesture and he lost his marbles there and then and ran to her. His companion did not dare look for him and left for home that very day. The next autumn when again picking mountain grass the folk saw the man again. He was now much bigger, but eager to chat, although he told them little of himself. They invited him to join them home and he was hesitant, but refused. On the third fall they met him yet again but now he was unrecognisable. He was now twice their height and wide as a horse.

'Do you believe in anything still?' they asked him with trembling voices.

'I believe in Trunt Trunt and the Trolls in the mountains,' he replied with a thundering voice.

That was the last anyone ever saw of him, and in fact, no one dared to pick on that mountain for many years.

All this one should bear in mind when wandering the highlands of this country, and indeed trolls are not the only beings you can meet. Ghosts roam the highlands, as do flocks of men that have abandoned civilisation all together and rob and plunder travellers for a living. Be careful, but remember this: many who have found themselves in peril against a troll have managed to survive by fooling it into being struck by the rays of the morning sun, as they turn them to stone. Some of them.

Gilitrutt

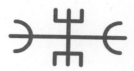

imagine, if you will, a neat little house built of turf and stone. Its triangular front lined with wood from a stranded ship's deck faces you as you approach. The roof is steep and covered with green grass but displays two little windows on each side with stretched cow bellies instead of glass to let a little light in. A door, so small that in order to enter the farmhouse you need to bow as if you are bowing before a jarl is in the middle of the tiny farmhouse and behind it a short hallway, a tunnel rather, keeps you bowed down as you make your way in. Your eyes struggle in the half darkness, the roots of the grass above stroke your back as you pass through the short tunnel. A kitchen, or a 'firehouse', with open flames licking a steaming iron pot in a hearth, meets your eyes on your left. Meat and fish are hanging above the fire for smoking. Food needs to be prepared for the winter and therefore a barrel of skyr, another barrel of butter, some cheese, smoked meat and fish and last but not least, a barrel of whey-pickled ram testicles, broiled sheep heads, cooked innards and other delicacies stands in a small pantry beside the fire house.

On your right is a small opening into the cowshed; in there is the stall for the two cows of the household. The sheep are too many to keep in there, they have a separate turf shed a few paces from the house, next to the small smithy. The horses almost never go inside, only in the worst of weather are they brought in with the sheep. The narrow tunnel then opens up into the living quarters of the people. The room is small, you can only stand upright in the middle of the floor and to both sides the beds of the inhabitants line the walls. Just above the short beds, usually shared by two, on a shelf are the meagre possessions of the people. Askur, or ash, the wooden food bowl belonging to each person, a wooden spoon, a small knife perhaps and may be even a book or two. Under one bed is a box of children's toys, sheep bones and jaws for animals, sea shells and other precious belongings tucked away when not being played with. In this room people sleep, work, eat, make love, cry, dream and perhaps tell a story on dark winter nights.

A young man once grew up in a house very much like the one we just passed through. It was a big house for the time, neither dank nor dark as many of them tended to be. In fact, this house was one of the bigger ones and even had the floor laid with wood from the same stranded ship as the front of the building. It was even so grand that the walls were covered with wood on the inside. The young man's parents were well off and hard-working people. They had farmhands, forty sheep and four cows, horses to ride, good farm tools, a big smithy, warm clothes and plenty to bite and burn. The young man grew up without a care in the world, spending his days riding horses and wandering about. Only every now and then would his father order him pick up a rake or a scythe and try and do a bit of work, but as soon as the old man looked away he would be on one of the horses or playing with the dog.

The years passed, one by one, and the young man's parents grew older, as we all tend to do. He had found his place in the smithy as a grown man and had little interest in anything else. In there he would spend many long days mending and creating tools and locks, hinges and scythes, building barrels and other goods for the farm and their neighbours as well. The old couple pushed him hard to find a young woman to marry, and as their only child, take over the farm after they had passed away. The young man was not at all without his good qualities; he had a sharp mind and a lovely voice and he was as handsome as an elf. It therefore did not take long for a certain young woman to catch his attention and soon enough the two were married and living on the farm.

Life was good for the young couple. The young bride spent her days riding her horses and basking in the Icelandic sun and the young groom rode along her side when he was not contemplating life and, of course, basking in the Icelandic sun. However, as we all know, nothing ever stays the same in this world. The day came when the old man spoke his last and not long after that it was the old lady's turn to join her foremothers. The responsibilities of the farm now rested on the shoulders of our young couple and to make a long story short, they did not live up to them. In a short time the turf houses, which required constant work and attention, began to sag and twist. The smithy the young man had loved so much became cold and little was done to secure hay for the animals, nor food or clothing for the winter. The workers, being ignored and frowned at, left one by one and eventually the young couple found themselves alone on the farm to take care of the animals and themselves. The winter that followed was a dreadful one. The sheep and horses fended for themselves, gnawing whatever withered grass they could find under the snow and the young couple ate what little they had left from the good days and whatever they could borrow from their neighbours. Weeks crept by and the love they had felt for each other withered away with the growing cold and hunger. When the first signs of spring began to show with the creeks slowly escaping the cold hand that had held them so tight and the light growing just a bit each day they resented each other greatly and felt nothing but cold in their hearts.

During one his rummaging through every house and shed on the farm looking for a scrap to eat, the young man came across a pile of wool his parents had sheared from the sheep a good while back, but not had the chance to spin into yarn. He thought to himself this was a job for his young wife, not for a moment thinking he in any way should take part. He brought the wool inside the house, dumped it in front of his wife and told her to have the wool spun fast and well. She gave him a cold look and not a word left her lips. A few days passed and the pile of wool sat untouched on the floor as a silent reminder of the state the household was now in.

One morning, in fact one of the first mornings the sun shone and most of the snow had melted away, the young woman was alone on the farm. A loud knock on the door startled her and woke her from her dreams of freshly boiled liver sausage and blood pudding. Slowly, and with great hesitation, she walked through the tunnel and opened the creaking front door. Outside stood the biggest, ugliest, scariest lady she had ever seen. Her clothes were thick and rough, her hair was like a pile of thorns and her voice was loud and shrill.

'I wonder if the young mistress has any work for an old lady,' said the shrew, adding, 'It will not cost you much, only a deal we strike between the two of us. No one will ever know.'

The young lady took a step back into the house and, to her horror, the old hag followed her all the way into the living quarters. There she sat down and opened up a pouch by her belt, took out from it a beautiful piece of fermented shark meat and with her knife, began to eat.

'I don't suppose you would want to join me?' said the old, battered thing as she passed a good-sized bite over to the young lady.

Hesitantly, she took the bite and sniffed it like a dog but her stomach groaned and grumbled and she soon ate the piece. Many more followed the same way as well as other goods from the old thing's pouch and soon the young lady was full, for the first time in a very long time.

Scared and eager to get rid of this odd creature from her house, the young woman pointed at the pile of wool and said, 'Can you have this spun before the first day of summer?'

The old hag laughed loud and hard and then said, 'Of course I can, and all it will cost you is my name. That you have to tell me when I give you the yarn on the first day of summer. If not, I own whatever is to be found under your apron!'

With that she grabbed the wool and rushed out of the house and was gone as quickly as she had appeared. Confused, the young woman checked the front pocket of her skirt and found nothing under her apron except an old key and a short piece of string.

As the days passed, the young woman grew more and more anxious. She had no idea what the name she had to give could possibly be. What was worse, a suspicion began to grow in her mind. On a particularly cold evening, late that very winter after having butchered one of their sheep and eaten a full meal, the young couple had found themselves in the same bed for the first in a very long time. On that night, they remembered their passion for each other and signs were now pointing in the direction of that evening having borne fruit. It seemed that more was hidden under the apron than an old key and a piece of string.

Names became all the young woman could think about. She paced restlessly around the farm, constantly muttering, 'Ása? Sigrún? Ragnheiður? Signý? Hjörleifur? No of course not, nobody can be called Hjörleifur.'

The day before the first day of summer, the young man was roaming the farmland, thinking hard about the troubles that lay before them when he heard a voice. He looked around, expecting to see some of his neighbours, a beggar or a traveller of some sorts, but he could not see a living soul. As he listened on, the words began to sound like a song and it even seemed to somehow come from the ground. He listened and he looked until finally he found a narrow split between two rocks, half buried into a mound that he had often played by as a child. He peeked inside the split and inside he saw a cave. A cave with a brightly burning fire in a hearth, dried and smoked food hanging all over as well as tools and other belongings he recognised as his own and his late parents. By the fire in the hearth there sat the most enormous woman he had ever seen. He was frightened beyond his wits but curiosity held him firm and he listened and looked for a while. A spinning wheel the big woman turned without a pause created a whirling tempo in the cave and she sang to the tempo. The song was crude and simple, all she sang over and over was, 'Housewife does not know my name, my name is Gilitrutt, Gilitrutt is my name, housewife does not know my name.'

With that he ran; indeed he felt like he was running for his life. He ran all the way home and out of breath and drenched in sweat he met his wife in front of the house. He quickly told her the whole story, her eyes growing with each word until she burst out in tears and flung her arms around the young man. She then told him her story and the two of them held each other in a way they had not done for a very long time. They looked each other in the eyes and kissed and the young woman whispered the news of the growing life into his ear. They kissed some more and then found their way into the house hand in hand and solved many of their troubles.

The following day was the first day of summer. Hand in hand they waited until a loud knock was made on their now-mended door, since the young man had for some reason felt a new wind in his sails the night before. He hid himself in the crawlspace behind the wood linings on the wall clutching a heavy axe, and his wife answered the door. In burst the old woman, looking even fiercer than before, threw down a sack of yarn and demanded to hear her own name.

The young woman struggled for words, her mind was blank and she could not for the life of her remember the name.

'Yes, uuum, is it Ása?'

'Ása is my name? Ása is my name? Guess again!' bellowed the old troll-wife (because that is, of course, what she was).

'Oh, well, is it Signý?'

'Signý is my name? Signý is my name? Guess again!'

Finally finding her courage, the young woman looked the troll straight in the eyes and said firmly

'Is it perhaps Gilitrutt?'

A look of shock and terror made the old thing even uglier as she recoiled and backed out of the house. As she went through the door, she fell on her arse and screamed in anger and frustration. Without a single word, she ran off, never to be seen or heard again.

Needless to say, the young couple now felt they had a fresh start. They worked hard for the following weeks over the short summer, side by side, and slowly righted their wrongs. Their daughter was born that autumn and became the apple of their eyes. Ása was the name they chose for her and she was a clever little girl. Slowly but surely their farm grew back to what it had once been, and their love for each other grew as well. They lived happily to a ripe old age, and if they are not dead yet, I suspect they are still alive and well.

Þórðarhöfði

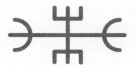

Þórðarhöfði in north Iceland is almost an island. How can something be almost an island, you might ask. Well, Þórðarhöfði is a cape, wide and overgrown with grass, and is a true marvel of nature. In fact, it almost seems like a small mountain rising from the sea, and is connected to the shore close by with a narrow stretch of land. Þórðarhöfði is the home to countless sea birds, which lay their eggs on narrow ledges on the vertical cliffs far above the sea, ledges that no fox could ever climb to steal the eggs to fill up their bellies. Men, on the other hand, have long since found a way to gather the eggs for themselves. They lower themselves from the top of the cliff on ropes and pick the eggs by hand, with nothing to catch them should they fall except the open waters and the rough beach below. In the old days in Iceland, knowing the land and sea when it came to hunting and gathering could mean the difference between life and death.

A group of young men were once gathering eggs from the cliffs of Þórðarhöfði. They were all from the farms in the area, loud and playful and eager to show the others what big men they were. They collected their share of eggs as they had been told and then found numerous ways to show their strength. They wrestled Glíma, an ancient tradition where two people face each other, grab each other's belt and then try to force each other to the ground without falling themselves. They sprinted, they jumped, they climbed and they finally took to throwing stones at a nearby rock face to test their aim. However, one of them, in fact the youngest of the group, took little part. His name was Þórður and he was a quiet young man, thoughtful, who usually kept to himself and was seen as rather odd by his fellow men. He lived with his parents on a farm named Þrastarstaðir and very much enjoyed the company of his grandparents, who lived on the farm as well. They told him countless stories from their lives and they taught him poetry, while he read their books of heroes past and learned from them the ways of the old country. Indeed, he read everything he could get his hands on and soaked up all the knowledge he could find.

The stones slammed against the side of the rock one by one, each leaving a white mark on the black rock and a smell of sulphur in the air. As the stones grew bigger and the young men's aim got sharper, Þórður, out of the blue, stopped their game.

'We never know who we hit or hurt with our stones and let us not throw a single one more,' he said in a loud voice.

The other fellows looked at him with surprise, they were not used to him speaking up, let alone in an angry manner like this. They laughed and scolded, 'What is the matter? Are you afraid of the elves or do you think there is a ghost in the way of our rocks? Do you think a troll is on its way to spank us?'

They pointed and they taunted but Þórður would not give up. Eventually they gave up and decided to call it a day. Þórður felt his presence was no longer wanted among the young men, so he quietly sat himself down and drank one of the fulmar eggs he had gathered from the cliff. He sat in the tall grass for a while and listened to the constant clatter of the sea birds until he got up and walked home.

The years passed as Þórður grew up on the farm. He said his goodbyes to his grandparents when it was their time, he grew tall and strong and kept to his work, but he remained a quiet man who walked his own path. One of his tasks as a grown man was to bring the finished products of the farm – spun wool, pickled butter, salted lamb meat and so on – to the Danish merchant in the village of Hofsós. For the goods he would then bring home such things as wheat and coffee, and perhaps even a little drop of Brennivín and a piece of tobacco.

Early one spring he set out on just such a trip, if trip it could be called since Hofsós was only a day's ride from the farm. He was lightly clothed and in a good mood as he rode off with the goods tightly secured on the back of another horse he led beside him. Halfway, the weather began to turn. The past days had been sunny and bright and the snow was fast melting away. Soon, however, Þórður found himself in the middle of a blizzard. A raging snow storm blinded him and took his breath away as he struggled onwards in what he thought was the direction of the village. He led his horses by the reins and walked blindly for hours to try and get some warmth in his bones and get to the fire that always burned in the stove of the inn at the village. He could feel himself growing colder and weaker with each step he took. Just when he thought he could not take a single step more, he found himself in front of a tall, painted door of the thickest wooden boards with big, brightly lit windows on each side. He knocked on the door and wondered which house he had stumbled upon. He knew he had arrived in the village and he knew every house in the village but this grand door he had not seen before.

'Maybe a new house has been built, Maybe I have walked all the way to the next town, or maybe I am seeing things here in the snow,' he thought to himself as the storm raged all around him and drowned his thoughts until all turned from white to black.

He woke up in a strange room in the softest bed he had ever felt. On top of him was a duvet filled with the lightest eider down and the pillow was as soft as a pile of cotton grass. He looked around to find himself alone in a brightly painted, wood-boarded room with a wash basin next to him and a chair and a desk against one wall. A beautiful wood cabinet stood next to the door full of books and scrolls and for a few moments Þórður thought he had, in fact, died and was now in a better place. As if in a trance, he reached for one of the books and began to read. He sank into the world of European knights and dragons, wars and valour, when there was a polite knock on the door. He put away the book in a hurry as the door opened and a kind-looking elderly man entered. With a smile he looked at Þórður and said, 'I see you found some of our books. Read away my good man, that is the least I can do to repay you.'

'Repay me? Who are you? Where am I? How could someone like you possibly owe a farmer's son anything?'

'All in good time, good man,' replied the man with a smile. 'Now you need to eat!'

Slowly coming to his senses, Þórður asked about his horses, but the man assured him they were in warm stables with the best hay in front of them and the farm goods safe in storage.

The man led Þórður through his house and into the dining room and Þórður thought to himself he must have stumbled upon a palace from one of the fairy tales his grandmother had told him. Every wall was painted, with pictures on each one, instruments, sofas, tables, books, lamps; he had never seen nor could he have imagined such splendour. He met the lady of the house, beautiful as the summer sun, and his heart skipped a beat when he was introduced to their daughter. She was the prettiest thing he had come across; her dress glowed like gold, as did her shining red hair. Her eyes sparkled green like the stones he sometimes found in the creek by his home.

'Welcome to our home,' she said in a voice that felt like a warm breeze. 'My name is Dröfn and this is my mother Ragnheiður and my father Stefán.' She offered him a seat by a long table full of the most delicious food, and the three of them sat down to a wonderful meal. Þórður sat by the table and ate his fill twice over, while listening to a conversation of humour and refined taste between his new friends. When they had finished the meal, Stefán turned to Þórður.

'I wish you could have met my son, but he is away running errands for us. He is a hard-working and a delightful young man like yourself, and he would probably not be alive today if it was not for you.'

Þórður could not utter a word, such was his surprise and disbelief. It was then Ragnheiður's turn.

'When you were a young man, just passed boyhood, you were sent with a few others to gather eggs from the cliffs. When they took to throwing stones you stopped them, even though they mocked you and laughed. Our son was there that day, and he got hit by one of the stones. He was knocked to the ground and who knows what would have happened if they would have kept up their throwing with the stones growing bigger and heavier. What you did took courage and we will forever be in your debt.'

Þórður stared at the three of them in disbelief and could not for the life of him remember a stranger getting hit by the stones thrown all those years ago.

'Now,' said Stefán, 'I believe you were on your way to do some trading. It so happens that this is a fine little town to do exactly that.'

They said their goodbyes and stepped outside the house, first gathering the goods Þórður had brought with him. It was still snowing heavily but nothing close to the day before and they could see from house to house. He now found himself in a beautiful town with colourful wooden houses, people he had never seen before on the streets, all of them handsome, tall and well dressed. Not a single turf house was in sight and the place was clean and tidy. They walked through town in the dense snowfall and enjoyed a good conversation on the way until they landed on the doorstep of a store. Inside was a world of its own. Þórður had never before seen such beautiful items, including silk, the whitest flower, the strongest tools, wine and candy, and again he wondered if he was indeed at the better place where he had hoped to one day meet his grandparents. He did his trading and got a better deal than he had done before in his life. Stefán helped him tie what he had from the store on to his horse and walked with him to the edge of the town.

○>╫╫>‹‹

The two of them now stood on a black beach and Þórður could hear the waves close by behind the wall of snow.

'Ride along the beach and you will find home. Thank you again my good man, and may luck follow you all your days.'

With that, Stefán turned around and left Þórður, still in wonder over his adventure. Again and again he pinched his arm and looked over to his horse carrying the wonders he had bought. He could not wait to get home to his parents and show them. When he had ridden for a short while it very suddenly stopped snowing. Þórður looked around and knew immediately where he was. He was riding on the narrow stretch that connects Þórðarhöfði to land, and where he could have sworn he should see the town he just left rose the snow-covered cape from the sea in its usual glory. Þórður set course for home and was greeted by his very relieved parents. They marvelled at the things he had bought and listened in awe to his story, knowing their boy would never tell but the truth.

Þórður lived to a ripe old age and lived a good and happy life. Luck followed him as he farmed and prospered and for some reason his sheep were the fattest and his pits full of hay. It is said that when he passed away, he left a few of his very unique possessions to his daughters and that these items are still owned by his descendants. The beautiful smiles, the red hair and the gleaming green eyes of his daughters are, as well, still passed on in his family today.

Of Hidden Folk

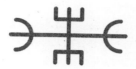

Elves are a peculiar part of our lore. Huldufólk as we call them by another name, hidden folk, and our paths have crossed with theirs for a long time. Perhaps they were already here, living in hills, mounds and cliffs when the first people arrived in the country to hunt walrus and seal and even whale. The first people in Iceland were dependent on the walrus, since it had the only hide strong enough to make ropes for the longboats that were one of the foundations of their culture. Maybe those people brought with them the first hidden people, whether they hid in the tales they told each other or on the very boats they sailed from the east. However they got here, they thrived in our culture for generations and still do according to some. Before me and Anna built our new house on the farm, I did sit down on the hilltop beside our house to be, one evening, and asked permission for the build. I never got any reply and took that as a yes. We have several examples of roads and buildings being repositioned after it is revealed that elven grounds are in danger. Whether we believe or not, we often show respect in front of the belief of hidden folks. To me, that is showing respect to those passed and the tales that taught, shortened the work and the dark, and explained what needed explaining.

The elves are a peculiar reflection on ourselves; often when we see them they are tall and well dressed, colourful and clean, bright and wise. On those occasions when we have been lucky enough to see inside their homes, they are described as bright and warm, clean and similar to the old turf farms, but have a sense of wealth to them. They eat well and they fair well most of the time, but they can be both very helpful and very cruel. They seem to be a better breed in some sense, at least we tend to look at them with a mixture of awe and even envy. They therefore rather reflect what we yearned for and did not have in times of darkness and cold, when food could be scarce and life hard on our island for most of us.

My grandparents on my father's side were Ólafur and Helga. They lived a life that some might call a primitive one today, a very small house to raise seven children, peat, coal and oil to keep them warm, a cow in a shed outside, a handful of sheep, the fish in the sea and the birds in the sky to feed them. My grandfather was a fisherman who took his boat out to sea every day and came home from his favourite fishing grounds with sometimes a boatful and sometimes less. My grandmother took care of the home and the children, no small job in times when every scrap of food and clothing was prepared from ground up and at home. She was as kind as she was patient, hard-working and proud and she brought her children up well. I am told that a fire started in the cowshed of their house from an oil lamp my grandmother had with her out there to provide her working light. Luckily it is a small village and soon people had formed a line from the little creek that runs just by the house and passed between them buckets of water to put out the fire. No one was harmed but the house was somewhat damaged. My father had moved to Reykjavík at the time to train as a carpenter and was given the news over the newly introduced phone that same evening. My grandmother told him who had done what and how everyone had their role and how all went well. 'But what did you do, mother?' asked my father, shaken and sad over the news, and she quickly replied, 'Me my boy? Well my dear boy, I started the fire.'

Just outside the small village where they lived, a great big hillock stands alone in the plains of the narrow fjord of Borgarfjörður Eystri and is named Álfaborg. It is believed to be the home of the queen of elves in Iceland. Her name is Borghildur and she is a magnificent woman. She has been seen numerous times, once even stopping by at a nearby farm, Jökulsá, to ask for a glass of whey on a hot and sunny day on her travels. When my father and his siblings were growing up they used to play all over Álfaborg along with countless of other children throughout the times. They were urged by their parents to play respectfully and not to climb the cliffs on the south side since those were the dwellings of the elves that leaned towards darkness more than the others. Granted, those cliffs are very high and coarse, but who knows, perhaps the dark elves do live there and are to be avoided. My grandfather passed away years ago and saw his last light in Gamli Jörfi, their 150-year-old cottage. It is as true as me writing these words that his last words on this earth were, 'There is something in Álfaborg.'

The Leg Bone

Reykholt in Borgarfjörður is a remarkable place. It stands in the middle of Reykholtsdalur valley, a beautiful, green valley where a river runs between hot springs and lush fields of grass and good people live and prosper. Nowadays, Reykholt is a place of scholars, artists and history with a wonderful museum and a thriving little town. For centuries it has been the centre of trade and culture, as it is positioned very well on an often-travelled crossroads that in the days of old linked north, west and south. The church in Reykholt was a very wealthy one in medieval times and was the centre of the village with corn barns, animal sheds and houses built all around it, and in the time of the great author Snorri Sturluson the village was even guarded by a wall. That, however, did not stop him from having his head cut off in the political turmoil after having written the *Edda* and other extraordinary texts, but that is a very different story. Over the centuries, the graveyard at Reykholt has been dug and redug over and over and it is not considered news of any kind that old bones turn up when a new grave is dug. They are treated with great respect and placed back in the ground, a tradition as old as grave-yards all round the world.

On one such occasion, a long, long time ago, four young men from the countryside surrounding Reykholt were digging a grave for an old lady that had passed away some days before. The four of them were good friends and even though they were carving out the final resting place for a kind, old woman, they joked and they laughed while they worked as young people usually tend to. The ground was soft and the digging not that hard at all, but the sun was shining and the men were hot and sweaty from the digging. They had found quite a few bones while they dug, but this was not their first time digging a grave in the graveyard so they made little fuss about a few brown bones.   Only on the rare occasion when they found a skull would they feel a little eerie, a slight chill down their spine, but none showed them-selves this bright summer day. They put the bones in a box the priest had given them and they knew that he would place these with the old lady, so they took care of each and every one. One of the workers, Finnur, was the son of a carpenter who lived with his wife and children a short way from the village. Finnur was on his way to becoming a fine carpenter himself and was a good young man. He was madly in love with a young farmer's daughter in the area, and used all the time he had off from his work to take his parents' horses for a ride and go to see her. Sigrún was her name and it was as sweet on his tongue as the ale his mother would brew every now and then, if not even sweeter. The two of them had talked about marriage and it was a thought that put butterflies in Finnur's belly.

When the young men had almost dug deep enough, Finnur hit something with his shovel. 'One more bone,' he thought to himself, and he was right, it was a bone indeed. It was a leg bone, a femur, and it was so big that it must have belonged to a giant. Finnur crawled out from the grave and measured the bone against himself. It stood as long as his hip from the ground and he and the other fellows could hardly believe their eyes. 'He must have been as tall as the church tower!' said one of them. 'Hey, Finnur,' said another one, 'this is a fellow who would look grand at your wedding!'

'Well of course,' said Finnur, 'I wouldn't dream of hosting a feast without this fellow!'

They laughed and took turns measuring the bone against themselves, marvelling the size and weight of it. They called the priest out from his study and showed him the bone. 'I have heard stories about this fellow,' said the priest. 'I am told his name was Grímur and that he was as fierce a man as he was big.'

He took the bone, as it did not fit in the box with the others, and took it inside the church. 'That is deep enough boys, I doubt old Rósa will be trying to make her way out of there.'

Old Rósa was laid in her grave, and the bones found with her along with the giant's bone, and in five years' time it was clear the priest was right about her. Finnur's and Sigrún's love for each other had grown over the years and they had now set a date for their wedding. A few weeks before the wedding, Sigrún had a strange dream. She dreamed that a man came to her, a very, very tall and sturdy man with thick red hair and a bushy beard. He looked sternly at her and she could hear his voice in the dream, cold and rough as the sound of rocks tumbling down a steep cliff. 'I am looking forward to the wedding, lass, and I sure hope you will have something prepared for a man such as myself!'

She woke up from the dream in unease and could have sworn she saw the back of the huge man leaving, hunched like a man against a snowstorm, down the stairs from the loft where she slept. 'Have you invited anyone to our wedding that I do not know of?' she asked Finnur when they met the next day.

'No my dear, only our friends and families as we have discussed,' he replied, and she thought nothing more of it. The next night she dreamed of the same man again, this time he looked angrier than before and said the same thing to her as the night before. She asked Finnur again when they met the next day and she was sure that this time she had struck a nerve. There was doubt in his eyes when he denied it, as he had done the day before. It was not until the third day, after the red-haired giant had come, angry as a raging bull, to Sigrún in her dream with the same words for the third time, that Finnur told her the truth. His voice trembled as he realised what was happening.

'I did invite someone. Five years ago I acted like a fool while digging a grave, and I fear I ridiculed someone we do not want at our feast, my dear.'

He told her the whole story of the femur in the grave-yard and of what he and the lads had said at the time. 'I fear this bodes nothing good for us,' was all she said, and Finnur felt she was right, as she so often was.

Sigrún was a clever woman and she knew where to seek advice. She went to see her grandmother, who lived a day's ride from her. The old woman greeted her grand-daughter lovingly, fearing that she had perhaps missed the wedding since her girl was here to see her. 'No dear grandmother, it is your wisdom I seek this time.'

They stepped inside the old cottage and soon had a little something for the soul in a cup each, and wisdom Sigrún got, and a handful of good advice in the mix. She rode back home that very evening and found her husband to be. 'My good man, you now have until the day of our wedding to build a house so big that it may house our unwanted guest. It is to be of the best making and of the finest wood and we will tent the walls on the inside with the finest cloth. Inside it you will build a chair and a table of strong wood.'

'I have to build a house like that in three weeks?' asked Finnur in a worried voice. 'That is going to require a lot of wood and a lot of turf!'

'Well, you better get to it then, if you are to marry me and have your life with me. It will stand next to my parents' house and there we will live out our days should we live long enough.'

And that was exactly what he did. He worked night and day, gathered driftwood from the white beaches of Akrar and cut it into beams and boards. Then he cut out turf in all shapes and form to form the walls of the great house. Incredibly soon he and his companions had a house built of such stature that few had seen such a one before. Not only was it big, but it was beautiful too, long and wide as the longhouses of the Vikings. Sigrún had woven the finest of cloth to line the walls inside and soon the house stood ready for a feast. 'Now we prepare our wedding to be held in the old house,' said Sigrún, causing her fiancé's heart to race for his throat.

'Now, why did I toil like that for us to hold the wedding in the small, old house?' he said angrily.

'This house you built for the big man, trust me and do as I say.' And that was exactly what he did.

Preparations were made and soon all was ready for the wedding. Two fat wethers had been butchered, salted and smoked and simmered in two great pots. Rye bread had been baked for a horde of people, butter had been churned for days, dried fish sat in piles, horse sausages hung in long strands from the ceiling and four big barrels of ale awaited their doom. Everyone was excited for the great feast, everyone except for Finnur who had a stone in his stomach and feared what might come. Sigrún now led him a few steps from the farm and asked him to gather some soil on their prettiest plate and pour some water in their finest cup. 'This you will carry into the new house and place on a table set for one. When your guest arrives for our wedding, you will get up and answer the door by yourself. You will lead him into the new house and offer him a seat at the table and have him begin to feast. You will then join us again in the old house and carry on as if nothing happened.'

Finnur did all as she had asked and it was time for the wedding to take place. The priest, now an old man, performed the ceremony and afterwards all the guests rode home to the farm and did the food and the ale the justice such wonders deserved. They ate and they drank and had a merry time into the middle of the night.

Suddenly, a very loud knock was hit upon the door. The door frame creaked from the firm hand that knocked, as did the whole frame of the old house. Every guest in the house fell quiet and looked to the door. Sigrún and her grandmother exchanged looks and Sigrún got up to lead her husband to the door. She than sat down again and continued to chat with her friends as if nothing had happened. Finnur opened the door with his heart pounding and thudding to meet the biggest man he had ever seen, the biggest he could have ever imagined. He towered over Finnur and said, 'Here I am for your wedding, Finnur, do you not remember me?'

'I do,' he replied, 'let me take you to your table.'

He led the man to the new house and invited him in. The man refused to enter before Finnur, but Finnur would not budge. 'I hope you will forgive me, but my new wife needs my attention,' he said, shaking with fear like a wet dog.

Eventually the man gave in and entered the house, saying, 'This meeting of ours should, perhaps, teach you not to ridicule the bones of those laid to rest.'

He sat down by the table and Finnur invited him to dine what was laid out. The man urged him to join him and sit by him but Finnur refused. 'Well, if you will not join me here, I guess I am going to have to make you join me in my own home instead!'

Finnur declined the big man's offer with a shudder and left him to dine alone. He went back to his wife and the guests who were startled and quiet by this visit, all that is but the bride herself. She smiled calmly and thanked their guests, who made their way home one by one until the two of them were left alone. When the last guests had left, they heard the familiar, harsh voice outside the window. 'I have nothing to thank for here, as I was given nothing but water to drink and dirt to spread.'

With that, he was gone. 'Now you are mine Finnur, and mine alone,' Sigrún said with a smile and the two of them together in one bed forgot all of the world's troubles until dawn.

The next day Finnur rose early with his courage restored and wondered about his guest in the big house. He was just about to step outside when Sigrún woke up and stopped him in the doorway. 'Now it is my turn, as I fear he has left you something to remind you of his invitation.'

She got dressed in a hurry and went over to see about the man. As she entered, she could see that the guest had drunk the water given to him but the dirt from the plate he had scattered all around the big hall for Finnur to step in. 'Should you have stepped in that soil my love, you would have been dragged to the grave with him and never seen a living soul again.'

She swept the floor clean and invited her husband to join her in their new house and he accepted, both thankful and relieved. Together they lived for many, many good years with their children to come and their children's children. They lived full and happy lives and never saw Grímur again for as long as they lived. Finnur built many fine houses during his days and even helped dig a few graves after that, but never once did he joke around with bones again. In fact, every time he saw a bone from there on he felt a cold shiver tingling down his spine.

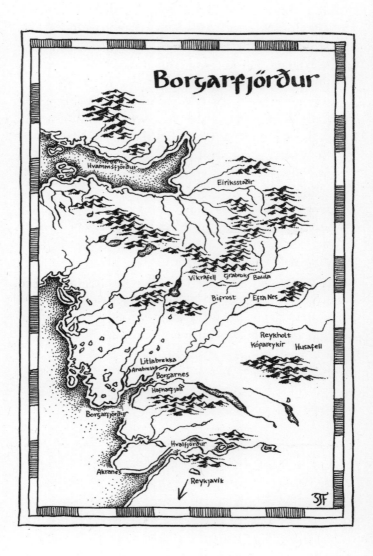

Borgarfjörður

Egill

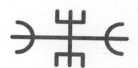

Egill was not a usual boy. His father, Skalla Grímur, was a chieftain, and a fierce one. His nickname, Skalli, was derived from a simple peculiarity of his, as he had not a single hair growing on his head. A berserker, he was nonetheless. A berserker is nothing to mock or play with. Such men would take on the form of a voracious beast when angry and could slay a horde of warriors in a single battle. They were most strong in the night, when the sun set, and were not to be angered in the dead of night. Such men were sought after by kings and queens and Skalla Grimur had his share of fights in his past. But let us get back to his son, Egill. He was nothing like a usual boy. He was as ugly as a troll, built like one, dark as coal and ill-tempered as well. He grew up in Iceland, at the farm Borg in west Iceland to be precise, where his father had settled after a voyage including several ships with his family, men, slaves, livestock and tools, chests and trinkets. Skalla Grímur, you see, had to leave Norway because of some hostility between his father and the king of Norway. His father was less than keen on taxes, as was Skalla Grímur himself. The difference between them and us is that they simply did not pay their taxes and picked up their weapons and polished their shields. And prepared their ships.

Skalla Grímur knew well of the land in the west where the sun never sat and crews of folk had spent summer after summer hunting for walrus. Those hides were simply the only one's strong enough to make a rope that held up on the ships. Everything else, even the toughest bull hide, snapped and broke, the sails went limp and the rudder was lost. He knew the island was big and mostly uninhabited, and that he could claim a massive area for himself if he moved quickly. He knew the existing law in that land was simple. If a woman chieftain wanted to claim land for herself, she had to bind a cow and whatever land she could cover dragging that cow behind her in a day would be hers. A man, however, only had to light a torch and run as big a circle as he could holding that kindle in his hand in one day. He knew that to be utter nonsense, as at least one woman had already successfully claimed a very, very big area for herself and was already quite well off there. He decided to play his luck. He and his wife, Bera, wound up in the west, where he would name his farm Borg, and we skip a few years.

We could spend many words on Skalla Grímur, his large area of land, his many men, the enormous stone he fetched from the depths of Borgarfjörður bay to use as an anvil, the fact my family farm (Ánabrekka) is named after one of his men as I live in the midst of this tale, but his son Egill is the one we want to focus on here. As ugly and ill-tempered as that boy turned out, he was also a brilliant poet. As the story goes, he followed his parents and their entourage as they rode to Álftanes for a feast held by Bera's father, Yngvar. His brother Þórólfur, who happened to be some winters older and a wonderful, bright and lovable boy, was also invited, much to Egill's dismay. Egill showed up at the drinking after ditching his babysitter and stealing a horse, following his family at the tender age of 3, yet as big as a 7-winter-old. He was seated on his grandfather's lap as he made his late arrival to the party. He recited some unforgettable poetry, far too high flung to depict in an ordinary book of folk tales, and received three seashells and a duck's egg for his efforts. His father, though, was less than happy as he had earlier explained to Egill that he was too young and too much of a mean drunk to join them.

As years passed, Egill became only uglier and rougher as his brother grew up to become a successful Viking and a sailed warrior. All manner of games were frequently played in those times, the sports of the era if you will. One pastime was to play a form of hockey on the frozen rivers in the area in the wintertime and Skalla Grímur enjoyed that game particularly. Leg bones of horses were tightly fastened underneath strong leather boots to make the ice skates of the time and the young men of the region would gather on the ice of the River Hvítá to compete. Egill was just as competitive as his father, only a tad crazier. Grímur was the name of one of the boys gathered and he was the son of one of Skalla Grímur's men. He and Egill went up against each other (Egill at the age of 7 winters, Grímur at the age of 11) and young Grímur proved himself to be a much better player than Egill. Egill was not used to losing as he tended to win every Glíma match and every fight he had ever been in, but Grímur was the better man on the ice. Not only was he better, but he had Egill lying on the ice after a tantrum and a fight that Egill lost. Egill solved that in a jiffy as he borrowed an axe from his comrade and buried it deep in Grímur's brain after losing to him. Skalla Grímur payed little attention to this roughhousing, but his mother, Bera, was deeply impressed and praised him as an upcoming Viking. Egill went ahead and wrote some undying poetry to mark the occasion of his first kill.

A few years later, when Egill was 12 winters old he was as big as a fully grown man, and then some. The game on the ice was still as popular as ever, but Skalla Grímur was not getting any younger. He was still a chieftain though, and a berserker by heart. This time, they would be playing much closer to home, in Sandvík, just a stone's throw from Borg. Egill and the very fellow who had lent him the axe that fateful day on the ice years ago, Þórður, were up against old Skalla Grímur himself. Þórður was 20 winters old and a fierce man of strength and agility. The pair of them got old Skalla Grímur close to defeat, but as the sun set, he went berserk, as was his way. He grabbed Þórður and hoisted him up over his head and slammed him down on the ice with great force. Þórður spoke little after that. He then turned to Egill and had the same fate in mind for his son. Egill had a nurse, a slave woman of his father's named Brák, who had taken care of him through the years and was one of the very few who actually liked a thing about him. She happened to be there at the games this winter evening and saw fit to intervene.

'You rage against your own son, Skalla Grímur,' she cried at her master.

The old man, still in his raging berserker mode, let loose his boy and ran after his maid. She sprinted as fast her legs could carry her towards the ness that still reaches far from the cove where they were playing. As she came to the point of the ness, she hurled herself into the strait between the point and a small island and swam for her life. Skalla Grímur picked up a boulder and threw it after the poor woman, hitting her between her shoulder blades. Neither came up, the boulder or the woman, and the strait is henceforth named Brákarsund.

That evening, Egill was late to the table at Borg. There, Skalla Grímur sat as usual with his horde of men, next to him his best man in arms and most trusted. When Egill showed up, he had an axe in his hand. Whether it was the same one as he used on the ice some years ago is not mentioned in his saga, but we can imagine it was. With a swift blow, he placed the blade in his father's most trusted man's skull and then sat in his usual spot to enjoy his supper. Both father and son felt the matter dealt with and turned to their meal. Neither one uttered a word to each other during that otherwise uneventful meal, and in fact not that whole winter.

The following spring, Þórólfur (Egill's brother, you remember, the fair Viking fellow) had his own ship in the bay by the farm. He was all but ready to sail east when Egill broke the ice and spoke to his father. Indeed, that was their first conversation since that uneventful meal.

'I want to sail with Þórólfur,' said Egill.

'Have you spoken to your brother about that?'

'I have not.'

'Well, ask him first.'

With that, Egill approached his brother and told him he wanted to sail with him.

'I see no chance of that happening,' said Þórólfur, clad in his fine linen and with a hint of a frown on his face. 'Your own father seems to think you are not suited in his own quarters,' he said. 'Why should I bear with your temper and trust you as we sail abroad? If you do not heed him in any way, why should I take you on myself and take the risk?'

'It might just occur,' said Egill. 'If that if this is your take on the matter, maybe neither of us will sail.'

That evening a storm grew, bigger and louder by the minute. Egill sat in his bed, muttering and whispering underneath his breath as the storm grew and he suddenly jumped to his feet and left the house. No one paid any attention as the people were merrily drinking the young captain's salute and his departure the next day. Egill found his way to where his brother's ship was securely tied to shore and boarded it. He then cut all the ropes that fastened the great vessel and jumped ashore before it drifted away. A worker saw the deed and ran to inform Þórólfur. His men jumped in a dingy and tried to row to the ship but the storm grew mightier as Egill's frown grew uglier. The ship wound up in Andkíll, a river's foot just across the bay, and was easily retrieved unscathed back to Borg.

When the ship eventually set off, Egill was on it and would follow his brother, to his delight and dismay. He became the Viking he himself had predicted and his story would unfold to be both long and great. We can all read about him raising a half-rotten head of a horse on the end of a pole to taunt queen Gunnhildur in the most foul of all dark magic, as well as him gouging out the eye of a stingy farmer to spew in the empty socket. We can enjoy the trickery of his daughter, Þórhildur, as she fooled her own elderly father into drinking milk as he was about to starve himself to death over the loss of his son, Böðvar, and we can read up on the silver he spread over Alþingi in order to show his fellow men they were mad about silver and nothing else. Although, maybe we need to ponder a bit about Alþingi and the silver in question. That was where the elite met every summer in the new established land that was Iceland. The meeting took place in Þingvellir for hundreds of years. It is a remarkable place that sits in our time between two geological continents and is a place of history and marvel. Still to this very day one can see the remains of stone-walled camps where the chieftains tented through the centuries as they flocked to the Þing to pass judgement or to plead cases. Great men bought their freedom and the poor were convicted there for centuries, with the very spots where men were beheaded and later hanged still marking the land. The pool of Drekkingarhylur, where hundreds of women were drowned for performing alleged magic or bearing children out of wedlock, still remains there as quiet as in those dark days. It is the site of the oldest parliament in all history, yet it is haunted with the tales of those hanged, chopped and drowned. All this we can read in the great feat which is Egill's Saga. But in the very end, let us have a look at how his son dealt with the oxen.

Egill had a son named Þorsteinn. Þorsteinn was a handsome man, tall and fair, with blond hair and a strength to him that had nothing to do with his father's. He was wise and modest and Egill never liked him very much. Ásgerður, his mother, thought the world of him though, and the two of them watched as Egill grew very old. Ásgerður lent her son cloaks of silk that had been given to Egill in his Viking times and were carefully kept locked up. They were colourful and dear and Þorsteinn enjoyed very much wearing them at Alþingi, where everyone could marvel at his good looks and beautiful robes. Egill discovered that Þorsteinn had worn the cloaks because he found them stained at the bottom when he himself had a peek at them one day. All he could say was that his son should better have waited until he was dead before mocking him by wearing such colours in the great Alþingi. In the form of undying poetry, of course.

By the time Þorsteinn was living at Borg after his beloved father, times had changed. On Ánabrekka, the next farm over, the times had passed as well and the fellow living there, although the son of Egill's friend, was no friend to Þorsteinn. Steinar was his name and he was wealthy beyond belief from his father's sailing with Egill. Steinar was a fierce and hardy man and he went out his way to step on Þorsteinn's toes. Every spring, Steinar would let his oxen loose to graze in the land of Borg, little to Þorsteinn's liking. This went on for two springs before Þorsteinn had his men watch over the borders between the farms and keep the oxen away. One afternoon, he walked to the top of a hillock above his farm and saw those pestilent bulls roaming his pastures once more. He grabbed his axe and went towards the bulls and the shepherd following them, a man by the name of Grani. As soon as Grani saw the well-clad, angry and colourful master from Borg approaching, he gathered the bulls and drove them towards home. Þorsteinn reached him at the gate of the wall surrounding the Ánabrekka farm and made good with his axe. He collapsed the gate stones from the wall on the corpse and headed home. The maidens in charge of milking found his corpse later that day but Steinar made little fuss.

Later that year, Steinar bought a tremendously strong and well-built fellow from a slave ship in Snæfellnes. The ship came from Ireland and the slave was as angry and fierce as could be expected from a man stolen by the tip of a sword from everything he held most dear. His name was Þrándur. He was given a big and bitter axe and the task of accompanying the bulls into Þorsteinn's land for grazing that very summer. One morning, Þorsteinn took a stroll with his axe between the mounds and hillocks of his land and met the great Þrándur. After a short attempt to explain the borders between the farms, the slave said, 'You are much less wise than I thought, if you choose to rest under the bitter blade of my axe. My weapon is far greater that yours and I care little about your greatness in comparison to the weight of my axe!'

'I am willing to risk that,' said Þorsteinn, 'you must see the wrong you are doing here man!'

'Just wait and see how much I fear your threats,' said Þrándur as he bowed down to tie his unbound shoe.

Þorsteinn, sick of his reputation as a weakling, raised his axe and severed the head of the mighty man in one blow. He buried the corpse on top of the hill they found themselves on and then calmly headed home. That hill is called Þrándarleiði, or the mound of Þrándur, to this very day and is right by the main road. The gate where Þorsteinn buried Grani is known to this day as Granahlið, or the gate of Grani, and is a stone's throw from our house today.

The tale of the bulls went on for years and did nobody justice, as feuds between neighbours tend not to. I urge my friends to collect their own evidence from Egill's Saga as it is a tale worth your time. It is mentioned in the very beginning of that epic saga that all now living in that region are descended from Egill himself. It is said that we bear a striking resemblance to him.

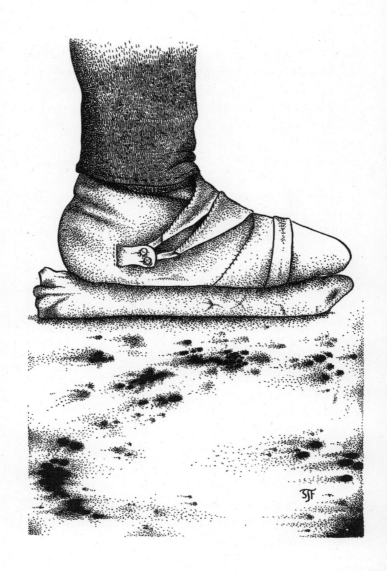

A Father of Eighteen

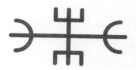

A very, very long time a go there stood a farm. It was a remote farm, far away from other people and other farms. It stood on the borders of the highland where summers are short and winters are long and hard. The farm was newly built by a couple who had worked hard on the bigger farms in the area for a long time, sometimes together, sometimes apart. They had scraped together enough to buy their land and build a farm with their own two hands. Maybe it was the beauty of the highlands that called them, maybe it was their urge to be independent from all others, or maybe it was both. But here they were, together. It was a simple household, only the two of them to do all the farm work, on top of building their new life so far away inland. They built their house on the bank of a small river that had dug its way into the ground over the centuries, and the banks provided shade for the trout that had lived there for as long as the river had sung. They could grab the trout with their hands if they lay on the bank, slowly lowering their hand, dressed in a wool mitten to get a good grip as the fish slowly swam towards them. The banks of the river were flat and green and the grass they cut with their scythe was tall and plenty, and they covered four big stacks of hay with turf they cut for each winter. They salted the fish, they smoked the meat from their few lambs, they made cheese from the milk of the ewes and the cow, and they fed the sheep, so making a difficult living for themselves.

They were happy in their own way, there under the mountains with little company except for the occasional traveller that rested their weary bones for a night and then went on their way for whatever the reasons that can drag someone up so far into the highlands. The two of them loved each other very much and one winter morning the woman knew she was with child. Her husband was thrilled, and afraid. Bringing up a child in these harsh surroundings would not be easy. Many children died young in better houses than their own, but it would be their child, and he wowed to take the best care of it he possibly could. The day finally came when the woman gave birth; and it was a long and difficult labour. After hours of agony she finally gave birth to a healthy, big boy who came into this world with his big blue eyes gleaming and gave a healthy, loud cry until he finally found his mother's breast.

The boy grew fast and, oh, did he grow. His eyes were the deepest blue, like the pools in their river, and he had the sweetest face his parents had ever seen. His hair was fair as frost on the grass in the morning and his laughter, which was heard throughout the farm each and every day, could melt the snow from the windows. He could walk and talk from an early age and his intelligence shone out of his eyes. Indeed, he was the apple of their eyes, although they had never, nor would they ever see or taste, the sweetness of an apple.

One morning, when the boy was still very little, his mother went out to wash some wool in the river. She had collected the urine from the cow for weeks and left it to go stale as nothing washes away the fat in freshly sheared wool better than stale urine. In fact, they say nothing leaves as good a shine in the long hair of a pretty woman as stale urine, but that is a different story. As she washed the wool, her boy jumped around her, singing and playing, and she told him over and over, 'Be careful my dear, do not leave my sight. Watch your step and do not fall in the river!'

She took her eye off him for a single second while she reached for some of the wool in the water and then looked at her boy. Her heart sank and her mouth went dry. He was gone. As if the earth had swallowed him, he was gone. He was not in the river, he was not behind the house, he was not in the smithy and he was not behind nor on top of the small hill that sheltered their farm from the northern wind and where he had so often played. She looked for hours and when her husband came home from hunting foxes for their skin he joined her in her search and sorrow. Throughout the evening they searched and the whole of the night until they fell asleep in each other's arms with tears streaming from their eyes.

They woke up next morning to a sound coming from the pantry. They jumped up from their bed and rushed in there to find their boy going through every barrel and pouch, every bag and shelf. There he was, as he had never gone, eating whatever he could get his hands on, and as soon as he saw his parents he gave them a frown and shrieked. His expression was grim, his eyes did not burn as bright and he spoke not a single word to his parents. The following days he wobbled around the house, kicking and yelling and stuffing into his mouth any scrap of food he could get his hands on. His parents watched him with a heavy heart, almost thinking it could not be their child. Indeed, he felt like a very different boy all together. The days passed, one by one, with no sign of improvement. The farmer had lost his patience and now stayed away from the house while the boy was awake, leaving all the work of taking care of what he now called 'the creature' to his wife. And what a daunting task that was. He ate and he ate, his manners all but forgotten, he spoke not a single word and grew fatter, louder and more difficult with each day. His mother's heart was broken and the days crept by in silence except for the boy's constant moaning and rummaging for food.

One summer morning, while the boy slept late for once, the silence was broken by a knock on the door. Outside the door stood a travelling lady, a wise lady, a völva. She looked the woman in the eyes and said, 'Something tells me you have a heavy heart and might benefit from my advice. For a meal and a good drink I shall tell you what you need to know.'

With a touch of fear in her heart, the woman opened up the door and let in the völva. To make a long story short, they quietly whispered into the late hours of the night with the boy trying his best to make out their conversation, but with no luck. When the völva set off into the midnight sun, the woman knew what to do. The very next day, she prepared to cook a meal in a pot. She made sure the boy was outside (she could hear him upon the roof shouting some gibberish at the sheep) and then began the cooking. She put some smoked lamb meat in the pot and placed it over the fire burning in the hearth. She then took out her longest ladle and her walking cane and tied the two together. To her walking cane she then tied the broom, and to that she tied the branch of a birch tree, from the kindling. This mighty contraption she then put out the chimney and the other end into the pot. Then she hid herself and waited.

It did not take long for the irresistible and wonderful aroma of the smoked lamb to reach the boy's nose where he sat in the grass on top of the house. He followed his nose into the house and stopped, with his jaw hanging, when he noticed the long wonder standing in the pot and reaching out the chimney. He stood there with bulging eyes for a good while, then walked back and forth in front of the hearth for another good while. He finally stopped, faced the hearth and said in a dim, coarse voice, 'Now, I am as old as can be seen on my cheeks, a father of eighteen children in the elfish world I am, but I have never seen such a long spoon in such a small pot.'

With that the woman ran into the fire house and grabbed what was obviously not her little boy. She put it over her knee and began to spank it on its bare bottom, again and again until the creature was wailing and wriggling like a worm on a hook. After a wee while she noticed someone enter the house. A tall lady, fair and proud stood there right in front of her, dressed in the finest blue linen with a stern look upon her face and her beautiful little boy in her arms. In fact, this was the prettiest lady, perhaps even the prettiest sight that she had ever seen. She stared at the lady and her glorious attire, and the lady spoke, 'Indeed we do things different. Here I am, pampering your little boy for weeks, playing with him and nourishing him, day in, day out. And here I find you spanking and beating my poor husband with all your might.'

〇‑‑‑‑

With that she put down the boy and grabbed the hand of what was now a small, hunched old man with a grey beard and a frown on his withered face. The pair left the house in a hurry, leaving the little boy behind with his mother. She embraced him with tears streaming down her cheeks, this time tears of joy and relief.

As the boy's father came home she told him the whole story and he was humbled and happy over his wife's good work and, of course, very happy to retrieve his son. He made sure from then on to cherish the two of them and soon the children in the household were two and soon three and soon four. The oldest had no memory of his time with the hidden people, in fact he grew up as good a man as he had been a baby. The farm prospered and luck followed the family on their journeys. And that is as far as I know the tale of the changeling.

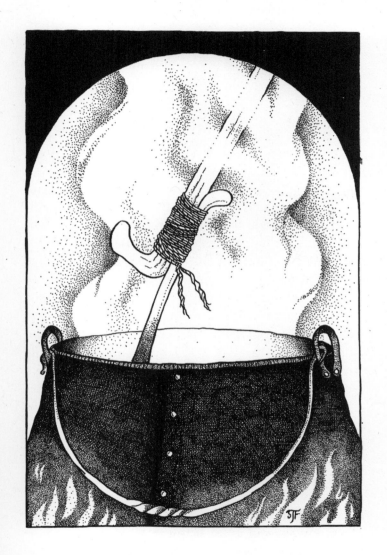

The Fearless Boy

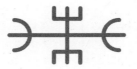

There once was a boy who was without any fear in his heart. At first thought you might think this was very much to his advantage, but it was quite the opposite. He was both ruthless and cold, as he knew neither fear nor love. His parents were halfway frightened of him as he grew up as he would never smile nor show respect to any living thing. They tried their best to tolerate and teach him, they even tried to startle him and scare him, to get him to feel, but all in vain. When he was of age, they asked their priest to take the boy in for a while, hoping that he could perhaps school him a little bit and help him find his way in life. The priest was curious about the boy and accepted, as he needed a worker on the farm since it was a big property and had many corners to sweep. The boy moved to the rectory and became one of the workers as planned. He proved himself to be a good hand but was always as fearless and cold as ever.

Time passed and the priest felt the boy to be intelligent in many ways and a fast learner. He did his very best to teach him compassion and love, but to no avail. One evening the priest decided it was time to give the boy a proper scare, to get his heart beating and to shake up his blood a little bit. He had the boy called before him and told him to go into the church and fetch him a book he had left on the altar. The boy listened without the slightest expression on his face and turned around without a word. It was a cold winter's evening as he found his way through the headstones in the graveyard in pitch darkness. He entered the church and began to walk down the aisle. As he did so, he stumbled over something on the floor and fell flat in between what he felt to be people, lying on the floor. That week, three people had tragically lost their lives in an avalanche, and their bodies had been brought to the church to be buried in the graveyard. These people, the priest had had gently placed on the floor of the church in their shrouds, as this was before the custom of building caskets for the dead. The boy got on his feet, but instead of gently stepping over the bodies, let alone being frightened, he took them, one by one, and threw them on the benches as he made his way to the altar. He then found the book and returned to the priest.

As he gave the book to his master, the priest looked curiously at the boy and said, 'Thank you very much young man. Did you find anything out of the ordinary on your errand?'

'Not at all,' replied the boy.

'Nothing that blocked your path then?'

'Nothing to speak of.'

'Do you want me to believe that you did not find those poor people that perished in the avalanche last week then?'

'Oh, you mean that handful of people that got in my way inside the church? I did not know you would make

⌖⟶⫿⟩⟨⪫

a fuss over that. They were quickly disposed of.'

The priest gave a look of horror as he asked, 'Disposed of? Whatever do you mean boy?'

'Well, I threw them on the benches as I kept falling over them. You wanted that ruddy book of yours, did you not?'

That was enough for the priest. He sent the boy away with a worried mind over that hardened soul of his and knew he could do nothing more. The next morning he had the boy brought before him once again and told him he would have to make his own way from there. He was given nourishment and new shoes, good, warm clothes on top and then sent away.

The boy saw no use in returning to his parents, so he simply decided to walk. He chose a direction and set off, not knowing where he would wind up nor what fate had in store for him. He went from farm to farm, slept in barns and sheep huts, ate what he could find or was given and had not a single purpose with his wanderings. Finally, he wound up in the south of Iceland, close to Skálholt, where the bishop of the south resided. There he walked through endless flat and grassy grounds under the watchful eyes of the ancient volcanoes in the area that slumber uneasy until they roar to life and spew their fire and ashes over the land, and sometimes even other lands. He asked to sleep in a cottage where only two old people lived, but they were glad to have some company and told the boy much news. There he learned that the old bishop had recently passed away in Skálholt and that the whole rectory was in a state of terror. A nasty ghost that the old man had kept under control apparently now went untamed about its nasty ways with no one to keep it in line. The boy thought to himself that this might be as good a way to get food and shelter as any, and set off the very next morning for Skálholt.

He could see the impressive tower of the wooden church long before he reached his destination. In fact, he was looking at the biggest house in the country and would for sure have been deeply impressed if anything could have stirred him in the slightest. He found the headman and asked for a bed and a meal in return for his work. The headman looked at the boy and liked what he saw, a tall and strongly built boy that could probably be worked hard on the many laborious jobs on the big farm. He was given a meal and then set to work, and he worked hard all through the day without uttering a word. After the workers had had their supper, the boy expected to be given wool work to tend to by the dim lights of the fish oil lamps, as was the custom of the time, but instead everyone prepared to leave.

'No one can stay here after dark after the old bishop died,' said the headman in a low voice.

'A ghost drives whoever stays here overnight mad and even leaves them dead. We all walk over to the next farm and sleep there in a barn.'

'I fear not the living nor the dead,' said the boy. 'Give me a bed and leave me here.'

After quite some bickering, the boy was given a bed to sleep in and was left to himself. The headman felt uneasy, as he had watched the boy work over the day and found him to be both productive and clever. 'Such a shame,' he thought to himself. 'That one could have been very useful.'

As darkness fell, the boy began to look around the house. He looked in every nook and cranny until he found himself in the fire house. He very much liked what he saw in there, fat shoulders of lamb hanging in the smoke, horse sausages dangling from the rafters and all other sorts of glorious meat. He had not had a bite of meat for a long time and ate his way through a whole shoulder before he grabbed himself a fillet of trout that hung above the hearth. As he was ripping the flesh from the hide with his teeth, he could hear someone rustling up on the roof next to the chimney. A deep, dark voice then said, 'Can I fall?'

'I do not see why not,' replied the boy, 'there is plenty of space here for you to fall upon.'

He had barely spoken the last word when something fell through the chimney and landed on the floor with a great thud. It was the torso of a man, both muscular and hairy. The boy merely glanced at it as he continued ripping the fish and chewing on the salt, smoky flesh. Soon he heard the voice again, 'May I fall?'

'Why should you not, there is still plenty of space.'

This time two long arms came tumbling down the chimney and landed on the great torso. The boy reached for a bit of bread and gave it his full attention.

'May I fall?'

'Well I haven't stopped you before, have I?'

This time a pair of legs landed on top of the pile as the boy was beginning to feel full.

'May I fall,' said the voice once more.

'By all means, I imagine you will have to see where you are going.'

And a large, very ugly head rolled on the floor and the bits and pieces began to wriggle about until the ghost stood in front of the boy with a frown as grim as a ram's behind on his face. The gruesome-looking ghost then left the fire house and went into the house.

⫷⊣⫶⊣⊰⊙

The ghost went all the way in to one corner and knelt there. He loosened one of the floorboards and took out a wooden chest and opened it up. The boy, who had followed the ghost with his belly now full, looked over his shoulder and saw a great hoard of silver in the chest. The ghost now began to rummage through the coins with his long fingers, digging and rustling, until he took a handful and poured over himself like a child playing in a pond on a hot day. The coins rolled all around the floor as the ghost kept on with his game, and neither one spoke a word.

When the chest was empty and the ghost had played for hours with the silver, he began to sweep it all into one big pile. Without the ghost noticing, the boy took one of the coins and put it in his pocket, and then watched as the ghost slowly filled up the chest again. When no more coins were to be found on the floor, the ghost started looking frantically for the last coin.

'Is this what you are looking for,' said the boy as he held the coin aloft.

'Give it to me boy, or you will regret it sorely, I have driven bigger men than you to insanity and then to their graves.'

With that, the ghost attacked the boy with a deep grunt. He ran towards him with his teeth clenched together and fire in his eyes, but the boy swung aside and let the ghost run with full force into one of the beams holding up the roof. A mighty crack shook the whole house, but the boy laughed. 'You are going to have to do a lot better than that,' he taunted the ghost and kept up his game for a good while.

'Give me the coin!' roared the ghost as he set himself up to finish the boy once and for all by crushing him against the thick, wooden front door of the house. The boy watched with a smirk on his face as the ghost ran towards him once more, with all the fury of darkness upon his face. Just before the ghost could flatten him against the door, he opened it wide and once more jumped aside, letting the being run and tumble outside into the first rays of the morning sun. There, with a mighty cry, he was swallowed by the ground and all fell quiet.

When the people returned the next morning, they were happy to find the boy alive and well. They asked him again and again if he saw something and what had happened, but he was silent about his adventures and went about his work that day. As the people prepared to leave the following evening, he urged them to stay and told them all was well, but they did not believe him and left as usual. The boy slept in his bed that evening and through the night, without noticing a single thing out of the ordinary. He told the people the whole story when they arrived the next morning and everyone was deeply impressed by his courage and felt safe enough to stay. The boy spent a few days in Skálholt and was praised and loved for his act of valour, but he felt nothing but boredom and decided it was time for him to move on.

This time the boy set off, again with nourishment and new shoes, to the mountains. He had heard stories of men living as outsiders in the mountains and wanted to see for himself what kind of life they lived, and even if they were there at all. He walked all the way up into the highlands, where he came across a lava field riddled with caves and crevasses. He soon saw a cave opening that looked deep and dark and decided to have a look inside. Deep down in the black cave he found seven sheepskins on the floor and a hearth along with supplies and other belongings. The cave was messy and unclean, and the boy spent the good part of the day clearing up and organising until all was neat and tidy. He then prepared a pot of stew for seven out of the meat he found in the cave and waited. When the cave dwellers returned the boy hid himself in the shadows and observed the men. They all bore weapons, axes and swords covered in blood and filth and they all looked exhausted and weary. Some of them had cuts and bruises and they were in a poor state altogether. They put down their weapons and looked around in the cave and wondered who had done them such great service. No less was their joy when they found the stew, simmering over the fire in the hearth, and they ate their full.

It was not until after they had eaten that the boy stepped out of the shadows and greeted them. With their bellies full and obviously knackered, they hardly raised an eyebrow when the boy presented himself, but asked whether he was the one who had cleaned the cave and fed them. 'That was me indeed, and I wish to stay with you for a while. In return, I can keep the cave clean and cook you a meal every day for you to return to, whatever it is you are doing out there.' All of them nodded in agreement before dozing off in the warmth of the fire.

When the seven got up in the morning, they hardly recognised the boy again. Soon though, the memory of the welcome from the evening before came to them and they looked him with approval and affection. The days in the cave passed one by one. Every morning the seven would rise before dawn and repair and prepare their weapons. They would then set off when day broke and return in the evening in a poor state, in fact they seemed weaker and more battered with every day that passed. Every now and then, one of them would carry home a swan or goose, or trout from the lakes, and the boy would use that to feed his new companions, who grew ever fonder of him with each day.

One evening, the leader of the seven sat the boy down by the fire and said, 'It is time we told you why we are here and why we must live out this retched life. All of us are men exiled from society for one reason or the other. We chose to live here and fend for ourselves here in the mountains, with our flock of sheep and hunting and fishing, and so we did for a good time until our peace was broken. We were attacked one day as we were out fishing in one of the lakes, and our attackers were not of this world. Three of them there were, and they seemed to appear out of the rocks in the lava around us, and their weapons were sharp and bit us bad. We were victorious that first afternoon, but much to our horror, they reappeared the very next day and now we must fight those three every single day in order to stay alive. With each day we are weaker, but they seem stronger as if something gives them strength between our meetings.'

The boy listened closely but said little. He made a good meal of goose breasts and neeps, and then went to sleep on his sheepskin.

After his morning work the following day the boy decided to spy on his friends. He kept his distance, making sure they could not see him, and watched as they were fiercely attacked by three swordsmen, who seemed to appear from out of the rocks surrounding the seven. He watched as a bloody battle took place, which his friends won with great effort, leaving them wounded and exhausted. They set off for the cave in a bad state, but the boy kept quiet in his hiding. When the seven were gone and all had fallen as quiet as it only can be between mountains, a figure appeared from within one of the lava stacks, a hunched little lady dressed in blue that seemed to the boy to be at least a hundred years old. She knelt between the three men and took out a jar of ointment of some sorts and began to smear it on their wounds and cuts. She even placed a severed head next to its accompanying neck and smeared the ointment on there. She then said, 'Rise my men, to fight another day!' and in front of the boy's eyes the men got up as if nothing had happened to them. He ran home to the cave but told his fellow cave dwellers nothing about his findings.

The boy followed his group of seven on their trudge through the lava towards their next battle the following morning and watched them barely survive. When they dragged each other towards home, he quickly grabbed one of the three swords laying on the ground and waited in hiding for the lady in blue. He was swift and ruthless as he jumped from behind the stack she appeared from and cut off her head in one blow. Her head rolled one way and the jar in the other. The boy grabbed the jar and could not control his own curiosity as he brought one of the three to life again, just to swiftly end it as the ghoul got to his feet. He ran to the cave to find his friends and much was their delight when he told them the whole story of the woman in blue. 'I will bet anything,' said the leader, 'that these were ghosts, awakened from their graves to revenge a wrongdoing one of us made in the past. Much have we bled on this lady's account and none of us will grieve for her, nor her three ghouls.'

The men healed well over the next days and weeks and their spirits rose with their recovery. Soon they had taken to practising their sword skills and fought each other in training every day. One day, the leader wanted to see for himself the effects of the mysterious ointment and simply cut off the head of one of his men out of the blue. They quickly brought him back from the dead and found in this the best of ways to spend their days. On one occasion the boy got his head cut off while training and his friends rushed to his aid. When the boy came around, the first thing he noticed was his own arse sticking out in front of him as his head was now attached the wrong way round. Panic ran through his veins and nerves as he tried to run forwards but went backwards instead. He turned his head from side to side, over and over again, trying to make sense of the world, but everything was upside down (or back to front) and soon he just screamed helplessly in fear and sheer terror. He was soon put out of his misery and swiftly made right again.

The boy lived with his group of seven for a good while, in the shelter of the mountains, but knew when it was time for him to return to other people. He said his farewells and went back home to his parents, who were happy to see their son again after all that time. He greeted them lovingly and took good care of the two for as long as they lived. They could hardly recognise the kind and gentle man that had returned to them.

Blackarse Hookride

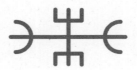

Once upon a time there lived a man and a woman in a cottage. They had three daughters, Ása, Signý and Helga. They were lovely young women and many a young man's heart skipped a little when they saw the three of them.

One summer's day, the old couple were out in the field gathering hay. This was such a small farm that they did not even have a horse to carry the hay, so together they raked it and bound it in bales, which the man then carried himself to the barn. He threw one of the bales on to his back after they had bound it and began to trudge home. Suddenly, he felt a great load added to the weight of the bale and his wife let out a scream. 'Who goes there, this is heavy enough as it is!'

'Never you mind who I am, but give me your oldest daughter's hand in marriage or I will crush you under this bale!'

The old man was not too keen on giving away his dear Ása to someone he knew nothing of, but the thought of being crushed was not too appealing either. He promised her hand and the weight was lifted. He turned around to face a troll, big and ugly.

'The name is Loðinbarði, father dear,' the troll said with a broad smile that revealed three dark brown teeth.

'Don't you worry, I can help myself,' he said with an even broader smile, with no more teeth to be seen. An awful stench filled the air as he turned his backside to the old couple and trotted off. The troll reached the cottage in a few steps and found Ása outside in the sun stacking peat for drying. 'You are mine now! Which would you rather, be carried or dragged away?'

'I am not yours, nor am I going anywhere with you!'

'Suit yourself,' said the ugly troll-man, and dragged her away, kicking and screaming.

They reached the mountains that evening and Loðinbarði closed the gates of his great big cave behind them, when he had dragged poor Ása inside. 'How do you feel now, still as cold and angry or are you ready to begin preparation for our feast? There will be many trolls and giants, so we need plenty of food and ale!'

'I am never marrying you, not for as long as I live,' sneered Ása at the troll.

'Suit yourself,' he said, 'there is more of you down there.'

He dragged Ása into a foul chamber and set her in a chair in the middle of the room. He tied her hands behind her back and he tied her hair to the back of the chair. 'I will let you ponder this for a little while, I suspect you will change your mind when you are hungry enough. Then maybe I will have more than one wife!' he roared with laughter and Ása nearly fainted from the reek of his foul breath.

The next morning, the old farmer was back in his field gathering hay. He was saddened beyond belief over the loss of his eldest daughter and worked with a heavy heart. He carried one bale after the other on his tired back into the barn, which was slowly filling up. He had just thrown one of the last on his back when he felt the same weight added to his shoulders as the day before. 'Is that you back, Loðinbarði?' he asked, but the weight and the stench gave it very much away.

The same scenario unfolded as the day before and soon the foul troll held Signý tight and asked her as he had Ása before 'You are mine now! Which would you rather, be carried or dragged away?'

'I am not yours, nor am I going anywhere with you!'

'Suit yourself,' said the ugly troll-man and dragged her away, kicking and screaming.

As soon as the cave door slammed behind them all went the same way for Signý as it had for Ása the day before. She wound up in the same chamber as her sister, bound to a chair with the troll slamming the door, locking in the two of them. They took comfort from each other, but both cried over their awful fate.

Helga helped her parents gather the rest of the hay the next day and closed the barn for the winter. As the three of them were about to head home for a bite to eat, they saw the massive troll-man return once more.

'Leave this with me,' she said to her parents, 'I have a feeling this is mine to mend and that I can find a way to bring my sisters back.'

She pushed her folk inside and faced the troll. 'This time I will not bother with asking your old folk,' he bellowed. 'Which would you rather, be carried or dragged away?'

'Well,' she replied, 'I would very much like to be carried. You look like a strong fellow and I suppose you would not find me too much of a burden.'

'Strong I am indeed! I have carried whole mountains on my shoulders and defeated the biggest trolls in the land with one hand behind my back. I am the strongest troll ever to live and my cave is the biggest of them all!'

'How impressive, my fierce troll. I look forward to seeing it,' said Helga with a great smile upon her face. He picked her up and strode in steps as long as rivers towards the mountains.

When Helga saw the awful inside of the cave her heart sank. It was absolutely filthy, with all manner of goods scattered all around the cave, leftover food on the floor and bits and pieces of who knows what, all in a jumble. It very much resembled a teenager's bedroom, but that is a very, very different story.

'This won't do,' she said. 'If I am to be married and live here I need to tidy up!'

She then began to clean and tidy with the troll-man looking on with a look of wonder on his face.

'Fiancé, I believe you need to gather food and ale for our wedding feast and invite your friends, is it not so?'

Astounded, Loðinbarði set off to do just that, but before he left he told Helga not to enter what he called his chamber of secrets. She promised, and he was off.

As soon as he had left, Helga opened the door to the chamber and found her sisters. She set them free and they were happy to see each other to say the least. They ate well from the well-stocked pantry and then cleaned the cave together, which was no small feat. When night drew in and the cave was cleaned out, Helga ordered her two sisters to crawl into a very big sack she had found in a very ill-smelling corner of the cave and told them not to make a sound. They were less than happy about this, as the pouch had contained salted herring before, but Helga insisted and they trusted her completely.

✶⟩⫴⟩⟨✶

'If the troll so much as puts the sack down, I want one of you to say, "I can see through hills and mounds!"'

The sisters promised to do so and lay quiet in the sack. When Loðinbarði returned with barrels of ale and food for an army, he was as happy as a puppy to see the state of his cave.

'What a woman you are,' he said, 'you will make a great wife!'

Helga smiled and replied. 'If we are to marry, you need to do me a service, fiancé. I have filled up a sack with the food you left around the cave, and since you are not having it, I want you to take it to my parents, as they are poor and can make good use of it. Leave first thing in the morning, but do not dare look inside that sack, for I can see through hills and mounds and I will know if you do.'

Loðinbarði was somewhat suspicious, but as he was not the sharpest knife in the pile and, eager to please his bride to be, he promised to do her bidding first thing the next morning.

At the crack of dawn, Helga kicked Loðinbarði out of the cave with the great sack on his back.

'It is heavy,' he said, in his profound wisdom, but Helga shooed him off and ordered him to invite all his friends on his way back home, as they were to be married that very evening. With a little hop and a silly smile, he left with the sack on his back. As soon as he was gone, Helga set the tables in the cave and prepared all the food he had brought. When everything was ready for a great feast, she took a tree stump used as a chopping block and placed it by the head table. She then fished a delicacy from the whey barrel, a boiled and pickled sheep's stomach, filled with sheep's liver and rye flour, chopped fat and kidneys, for you see, the Scots are not the only ones in this world to eat such wondrous things. She placed the bloated sausage on top of the tree stump and carefully covered it and the stump in a white cloth she had found in the chamber, no doubt stolen by the foul troll. Before running out the door, she smeared her face and clothes with the ashes from the hearth and made sure to blacken her golden locks as well. She then grabbed a hooked staff and ran for home.

As Loðinbarði made his way to the farm, where he had raised havoc before, he grew tired of carrying that sack on his back as he was dead lazy by nature. He stopped behind a mound and set down his weight to rest. A soon as he did, with full intention to look in the sack, he heard a voice. 'I can see through hills and mounds!'

'Well, in that case, I better not look, as my bride to be might get angry with me. What a clever woman I am about to wed,' he thought to himself and shouldered his burden to carry on his journey.

His ugly face was not what the old couple most wanted to see as he threw down the sack on their door-step, but much was their joy when he stormed off and they looked inside.

All the trolls and three-headed giants he met and invited on his way home to the cave accepted his invitation. Soon, he had a herd of awful misfits with all sorts of heads, heading to his cave to celebrate his wedding. Each and every one had heard of this wonderful woman he was about to marry and was eager to see her and drink and eat endlessly. They all rested under a great black cliff to share a sip of each other's flasks, each as big as barrels. The lot of them were wonderfully drunk as they set off again, when they met a tattered little thing, filthy and black as coal, riding what seemed to be a hooked staff.

'And who might you be, you tiny little thing?' asked Loðinbarði, leading the pack.

'My name is Blackarse Hookride,' replied the tiny creature, 'and I come from the mountains.'

'Aha!' he roared, shaking loose a few rocks in a nearby mountain pass. 'Did you by any chance come across my mighty cave?' asked Loðinbarði of the tiny speck in front of him.

'Well, yes I did. It was open and I peered inside, only to see tables set for a feast and a bride, patiently waiting by the head table.'

They all roared with laughter and could hardly wait to get to their drinking and fighting. Soon, the lot of them reached the cave and made good with the food and the ale.

Loðinbarði, of course, set himself next to his bride in white and began to eat and drink as soon as the lot reached the cave. She was quiet, to say the least, but he did not mind at all. In fact, he was very happy with her sitting there all silent as he and his friends ate and drank, and so the night wore on. The ale he had stolen was strong and the food he had stolen was delicious. He kept his eye on the motley crew he had gathered, as they grew louder and drunker.

'What do you want, Leppalúði,' he asked one of his mates as he sat down next to the bride.

'Nothing more than to congratulate the lovely bride, and perhaps to snatch a look at her,' said the tremendously ugly troll-man that had sat himself on the bench at the high table. He gave the bride a tap on the shoulder, only to have her head rolling on to the floor. The pair of them looked at each other in horror.

⚬⌐ᚲᚻᛁᛁᛁᚲⲟ

'You have killed my bride, you foul ogre!' shouted Loðinbarði. 'For this you will pay dearly!'

They drunkenly stumbled to their feet, only to find that the bride was a little more, or less, than they had expected. 'You have made a fool of us all Loðinbarði! This is no woman, but a liver sausage and a tree stump!'

With that, Leppalúði grabbed the sausage from the floor and devoured it in one gulp. The following was a tremendous fight between trolls. No human could ever imagine such a brawl. The rivers in the mountains turned thick and brown as the glaciers broke up from the quakes and crumbled into them. Whole mountain tops came tumbling down the sides of their very own mountains as they shook from the magnificent rage that broke out in the cave. Some sided with Loðinbarði, others sided with Leppalúði, and others sided with themselves to finally enjoy a good fight. Interesting things are far apart with the trolls, and this was a feast to their liking. They fought and they fought until they had fought each other to the bitter end. A foul heap of troll-men soon lay on the cave floor, each as dead as the next.

Helga travelled that whole day and the next. When she finally reached home her folk could hardly recognise her through all the filth that she had disguised herself with and the dust from her travels. They greeted her well and bathed her and fed her well. The three sisters waited for a good, long while until they ventured back to the cave. What they found there is best left to the imagination, but they did gather all sorts of wonders from within to bring back home, and made more than one trip to recover all they had collected from the hoard. As they returned home for the last time, black, thick smoke rose towards the sky through the opening of the cave.

As far as I know, the three of them fared well and took good care of their old folks, for as long as they counted days. What they gathered from the cave was a mighty treasure and they all made good use of what Loðinbarði left his dear bride until their last day.

A Few Odd Men in the East

*T*he isolation and the glorious landscape of Borgarfjörður Eystri has created some outstanding characters and still does to this very day. The fjord is wide and open to the sea winds, and the flatland in the valley beyond the beach accommodates a village and several farms between the mountains. The beaches are of black sand and the most colourful pebbles you can imagine, polished for ages and ages until they become as smooth as a child's cheek. Jagged rocks separate these beautiful strips of beaches and greet the waves created by the howling north east wind by hurling them full of sand and seaweed over the village, which stands a road's width from the sea. Beyond the village, green plains stretch far and wide with a silvery river winding from the inner most part of the valley all the way to sea. Trout and salmon find their way up the river, in the past occasionally met by a dangling worm or even a bit of net that has been placed in the cover of night. It was the custom to use every way possible to gather food, and salmon and trout are good food even though the river is off limits sometimes. Over all this, the mountains stand their guard. Tall and steep and in every colour of the rainbow they rise from the flatlands, rhyolite slopes giving them all these magnificent colours. Some of them look like bowls upside down with their oval tops and gentle hills, while more of them reach for the heavens with piercing tops that make you feel like you are walking on thin air when you have reached them.

Benóný was the name of a fellow. He lived in Hvalvík, a remote, narrow and jagged cove, and his first year he spent with his wife in a narrow cleft with a tarp stretched across it for a roof. No one has ever lived in that bay, neither before nor since. He built all sorts of contraptions and was an engineer by heart. He once built a rowing machine to fit next to him in his dinghy, driven by the wind itself. After carefully fastening it to the thwart in his boat, he sat next to it and set off, determined that from there on he would have a mate that would never give in and could row until the end of time. The pair made their way to the middle of the loch, only for the wind to pick up on that fine summer day. The mechanised rower sped up, as did Benóný. The wind then turned to a strong breeze and Benóný rowed even harder. Soon, he was rowing for his life as the boat circled around and around and Benóný was just about to give up to the constant madness of his relentless partner. Amazingly, no one knew how to swim in those days of rowing open boats toward the horizon, but Benóný was nonetheless ready to throw himself overboard when the wind suddenly calmed down. He aimed the boat to shore and stepped ashore very much alive. With a mallet he smashed his creation to bits, claiming that the Devil himself had sat next to him that day on the sea.

My father's people have lived in that fjord and in the coves and bays that line the coast south of the fjord for a very long time. They lived off the land and off the sea and life could be hard in these remote places, make no mistake. Those people had to be hard working and creative to survive. Perhaps they grew to be a little bit eccentric, peculiar even over time, but that is for the better, not worse. Without peculiarities our lives would be dimmer, and were we all to be from the same mould things would be a lot less fun in this world. Stefán was one of these people. He lived in a house called Úranía in the village in the nineteenth century and was skilled in many trades. He could forge iron as easily as he joined timber, he built boats and houses as well as mending clocks and sextants. Too soon, he even cast his wife's headstone. He did so in concrete and it is a beautiful stone, with the print still readable and can still be seen in the old graveyard where the church used to stand. I have heard my father, who is a master carpenter by trade, say that if we are handy in any way or form, it is from this man that it comes from. His anvil is in my father's wood smith and is used often.

Another one was my great-grandfather, Ágúst, who towards the end of his time lived alone in his house Tunga, just by the sea and in the middle of the village. One day during the war a naval mine was spotted floating in the sea, uncomfortably close to land. Much of the village was evacuated and people took cover in the school, except for Ágúst, who was not about to leave his home for some measly stick of dynamite bobbing in the water. The explosion was powerful to say the least when the floating mine touched shore, windows shattered all through the village, doors were askew and things broken and scattered all about. When his friend reached his house he met the old man in the hallway of his small house with the front door in his hands.

'Are you OK?' he asked the old man in a worried tone.

'What is all this fuss about?' asked the old fellow. 'I was just about to have a look at the mine when the front door came hurling at me and threw me against the wall!'

It is very likely that the door acted as a shield and maybe even saved his life. Lucky for him, and lucky for me. I am very thankful for that door being as sturdy as it proved to be.

Jóhann was another one who tied different knots than his fellow men. He was my great-grandfather as well, and could tell the weather for upcoming months by making three cuts, lengthwise in a spleen, from a freshly slaughtered horse and leaving it to dry. What he saw in those cuts we have no idea, but he could be very accurate in his weather forecast, people say. He was a farmer and lived on a farm just outside the village, named Ós. Bad luck struck one time when he was feeding his sheep in the barn as he managed to break his finger quite badly. The joint in the middle of the finger was all but ruined, the finger flapped lifeless and he found himself in a pickle. There was no doctor in the village and the nearest one was many, many hours or even days away. He was no stranger to walking long distances, in fact he was known for his endurance and was often asked to fetch medicine in the wintertime when all the passes in the mountains were full of snow and there was no way to get a horse over to the nearest town. On one such a trip he was forced to bury himself in snow and sing for two days while a raging snowstorm bellowed over his lair. An angry, hopeless man cannot sing, you see. Some say such perilous trips were not only made to save lives by fetching much-needed medicine and thus even saving lives, but also when tobacco and spirits had run out in the fjord. What is life without a little spice?

Well, this time he thought that a walk to the doctor would do no good. The damage to the joint was too severe and the long time until he would receive treatment would do nothing to aid its chances of recovery. He therefore set his finger on the manger and took out his trusted pocket knife, as always sharp as the mountain edges surrounding him. With one swift cut he performed a simple operation right there in the barn, then disinfected the wound with tobacco from his pouch and dressed it with his handkerchief. This took care of the medical side of his predicament but he was now faced with another. What is a man to do with a severed part of himself? Is this an occasion to involve the priest? Are there any sort of arrangements needed to make sure the stub follows you into the afterlife should there be one? Should a tiny grave be dug and a ceremony be held in the church in front of the whole congregation or a hole simply dug in the ground outside the barn and nothing more? Much to his relief, in the midst of all these deep theological and philosophical ponderings, his dog came running home from one of its many trips around the farm to make sure it had peed on every rock and mound. The dog happily accepted the treat and the problem was gone.

Some of the more memorable characters from this part of the land were the brothers from Höfn. Höfn is a farm in Borgarfjörður Eystri, on the east side, and sits a stone's throw from the shore. The two brothers, Jón and Hjörleifur, grew up with their father, Árni, and were very big in all manner of speaking right from their early years and known for their unusual strength. The three of them fished for shark to draw from its liver the potent and powerful oil used to fuel lamps. They made their living by selling the oil, but made sure to reap its benefits themselves as they drunk at least a pitcher full of it every day. Surely this contributed to their enormous strength and kept them both fit and healthy. Back in those days, not a single thing caught was made to go to waste and the rest of the shark they prepared and sold as well, apart from what they feasted on themselves. The flesh of the shark is a delicacy when ready to eat, strong and odorous, but unfortunately it is also quite poisonous when the shark is fresh. It is therefore cut into thick strips and buried in gravel for a few months, which lets out the ammonia that is both poisonous it and gives it the wonderful flavour as well as starting a fermenting progress in the flesh itself. I urge you to try it. Shark was the brothers' livelihood and the sea was their workplace.

The brothers were liked in the community, but seen as rather odd. It is said that Hjörleifur spoke in an unusual manner, slowly and sometimes said the strangest of things, but still had a very good grasp of the language. When he heard of the drowning of a doctor who happened to be a good man from two fjords over he said, 'The silver basin sinks in sea while the broth cups stay floating.'

The brothers even dressed in a strange manner. They tended to wear shorts in every weather and throw over themselves coarse, black woollen jumpers that reached down to their knees. This they would tie up with a braided strap they called 'the strip of turf' and top everything off with a blue woollen cap. Hjörleifur always carried a great, thick staff with a heavy iron pick attached to the end. Although a very calm man, he could explode like an avalanche when angry. He is said to have aimed his staff at someone who managed to offend him one time and came all too close to spearing the man like a cod hoisted from the ground before his brother stopped him and calmed him down.

A man named Þorsteinn lived on a cottage on Hjörleifur's farmland and lived poorly, but the brothers made sure he never starved and let him have a roof over his head. This fellow once got very angry with Hjörleifur and hit him over the head with a shovel. Hjörleifur grabbed the man, heaved him up above his shoulders and threw him like a sack of rye a good way. The man came down hard and did not stir for a long while. Hjörleifur thought he had killed the man and instantly regretted his temper as he so often did when it led him astray. He was very relieved when the poor bugger got to his feet, and to Þorsteinn he said, 'It was not meant to be this far!'

One fine day, the brothers rowed out far and set out their line and hooks. The bait was rotten horse meat, the line was thick as a finger and the hooks were big and sharp as you would expect, given that a shark is no light-weight. They soon had caught an unusually big one and even Hjörleifur had to struggle to draw it to the surface. Just before he managed to drag the shark in to the ship, the line broke. He swiftly grabbed the tail of the monster with both hands as it was swimming away and pulled it towards him. He pinned the tail fast under his right arm and said to his brother, 'It seems I am not rowing this time. Do you mind getting us home?' Jón took the oars and rowed the ship built for eight rowers home, pulling the massive shark along held the whole time by

Hjörleifur. As the boat touched land, the two of them got out. 'Which would you rather then brother, sharpen the shell or save the sardine? Hjörleifur chose to get the ship in the naust and hoisted up the bow as his brother picked up the beast of a shark. They both finished their work in peace and quiet, as was their way.

On another occasion the priest in the community got into a bit of trouble. His name was Hjörleifur as well. One fine day the sun was shining its brightest and the priest had all his people gathering hay on the fields. His wife was there as well, binding hay bales paired with one of the workers. She had left every door on the farmhouse wide open to let in the warmth and fresh air. This was a necessity since the turf houses tended to get quite damp if not kept properly dry by letting in air. The priest, of course though, had other more important things to do and stayed at home that afternoon, no doubt to contemplate mortality or write his next sermon. He sat by a table in his study and was startled to say the least when he heard furniture thrown about, deep grunting noises and then someone very, very large pounding voraciously against the support beams of the roof as if willingly trying to collapse the whole structure. He quietly got to his feet and peeked into the tunnel to find himself face to face with his own bull. It was an old bull and not a very polite one, and it was known to attack people when in a foul mood, even a holy man such as its owner. Hjörleifur was a well-built man, not quite as strong and big as his namesake, but still a very well-built man. He immediately bowed and got his shoulder under his bull's head and began the wrestling. The pair of them saw the inside of the common room, the fire house and even the pantry before the good priest finally managed to get the bull out of the house. He was exhausted after the struggle and sat himself down on the side of the house. He managed to catch the attention of one of his workers, who immediately came running. His worker opened up the stables and after the priest had caught his breath the two of them were able to herd the raging bull inside. Not only did they close the door behind the thing, but placed rocks against it as well to keep it well secured inside. That very evening, when the priest had recovered from his adventures with his bull, he had his worker bring word to Hjörleifur.

He arrived in the crack of dawn to take care of the bull. He brought with him a long blade, specifically made to cut up shark meat. It was a thick and strong blade with a rough wooden handle, very familiar to its owner's hand and Hjörleifur looked like a troll wielding a sword as he asked his priest, 'Where is the calf then?'

'In the stables,' his namesake replied, 'and I want you to kill it. Do not waste the blood though, a maid will join you with a trough to collect it for blood pudding.'

As soon as Hjörleifur had removed the rocks from the door and opened it a sliver, the bull came charging. He grabbed it by the horns and the two of them danced around between the farm buildings for a while. Eventually, he had the bull taken care of, although no blood pudding could be made after their struggle.

Hjörleifur had a son late in life and named him Árni. The pair of them were once by the harbour in the village as Árni was helping to unload a merchant's vessel. The young man carried a barrel of wheat under each arm up the beach while his fellow workers took one between their arms.

'This is how I carried them when I was your age boy,' said Hjörleifur with a deep sense of pride.

'There is still room for more,' replied the young man.

Gathering food was essential when my father and his siblings were growing up, and my grandfather, Óli, was good at just that. He was a hunter by nature as well as being a fisherman his whole life and he had a one-shell Swedish shotgun about the size of a cannon. He would load his own shells in their cottage in the evening, carefully measuring the powder and counting the pellets in to each one. When off hunting ptarmigan and all sorts of sea bird, he would never take a shot with only one in range; shells were expensive, as was the powder and the pellets. Two or more should always be lined up to make the most of the shot. He was a true lover of tobacco and smoked pipe and cigars for decades.

One crisp winter morning he and my father, 13 years of age, set off for the heath beyond the flats of their valley to hunt for ptarmigan. They had not ventured very far when my grandfather felt the need for his ritual. He pulled out his pipe and the pouch of leaves and carefully, yet with quick manner and trained fingers, stuffed the bowl full. He then reached for the little case of matches always kept in his shirt pocket by his heart. This time, the pocket was empty, though. He immediately began searching through every pocket, trousers, jumper, coat, but found no matches. He emptied the knapsack he carried on his shoulder and the knapsack of his son just in case. It became ever more obvious that matches had not joined them on this particular hunt. Daylight is short in the midst of winter in Iceland and my grandfather was not about to turn back. They trudged on in the snow to continue their collecting of food for the household.

Every now and then throughout that entire day they stopped as my grandfather went meticulously through their gear in search of fire, every time coming up short. They had a good day of hunting and carried a good bunch of birds each towards home as the day wore on. As dusk fell, they were about halfway to the village. Óli had held up remarkably well but was indeed looking forward to getting home and enjoy a well-earned pipe. As the pair of them could make out the lights in the windows in the village, they met one of my grandfather's companions. Little was spoken before he dropped the obvious question, 'Do you have a light my good man?'

'Are you wandering around smokeless my friend? That is awful. I can do better than a light,' his friend replied, and he took out a cigarette. He lit the thing, said his goodbyes and handed the flare to Óli. The friend went along his way and was swallowed by the falling darkness. Óli managed but a single puff before he stumbled flat over a stretched fence wire, falling face flat in the snow and putting out the small burning. As he got to his feet with the broken, lifeless twig between his lips, he said nothing but carried on home with an expression of utter disappointment on his face.

Crossroads

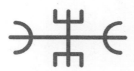

Old Year's Eve and New Year's Eve are nights of mystique. According to old tales, cows can speak on New Year's night, and if you listen in, you will be much the wiser about great many things. That is, if you do not lose your mind in the process, which is very much a possibility. The hidden folk dance on Old Year's Eve, often around bonfires, and their festivities are often seen by men. They have the best of times and are glorious to behold in their silk and satin, and it is no wonder people have often wanted to join in and even done so. No one should, however, approach those dances as the elves are not to be trusted, no matter what splendour they might offer. The price to pay can be more than you can afford, and many have never been seen or heard from again after joining in the festivities of elves. It is believed that the powers of hidden folk are the most potent on New Year's Eve. Not only are they particularly dangerous to come across then, but it is also the time of year when the working elves move from farm to farm much like people do in summer. It is therefore the most likely night of the year to meet hidden folk, but some ground rules must be kept in mind should you find yourself on a walk in the Icelandic countryside on New Year's Eve.

There once was a man named Fúsi, who was a farm worker and had been for his entire life. He had no memory of his parents nor of the farm they had lived on and he was born on, he only knew that he had been but a toddler when his father died and the home broken up. His mother had died a few years later he knew, a worn-out, overworked shadow of the woman she once was. Fúsi's life was not an easy one to say the least. As a child he had been constantly moved from farm to farm, as was the custom of the time with orphans. As a matter of fact, whichever farm that was willing to accept the least payment with each orphan was the one to house him or her for the coming year. That way, officials could pay the least amount possible with each orphan, each cripple or the old, but it most certainly did not mean they always wound up in the best of care. This, Fúsi had felt on his own skin over the years. Sure, there had been better times in between but most of the farms he had seen provided little food and poor housing as the people were poor themselves and sometimes even mean. Fúsi was now a grown man, had hired himself as a worker on one of the bigger farms in the county and was neither happy nor unhappy.

Fúsi knew what it was to be hungry. He had starved before, both as a child and an adult, and he could not resist the smell or sight of food. His mistress caught him every now and then snooping around in the pantry when he was supposed to be out working, for he always felt hungry, even when he got a bite of meat in his bowl or an extra ration of porridge or skyr. He was a good worker, though, and his masters forgave him for his snooping as they were decent people and liked Fúsi despite his quirks.

One evening, approaching new year, Fúsi and the rest of the people on the farm sat by the dim lamp light and worked wool. The younger ladies were knitting and the mistress spun the wool on her spinning wheel. The men combed and felted, and as they worked they shared stories. Fúsi was not much of a storyteller himself; truth is, he did not care too much for stories of ghosts and trolls. Having spent his share of time in the darkness, he was certain there was nothing in the dark to fear but the ill doings of other men. He had also roamed the heaths and highlands often enough to know that trolls were scarce, if they existed at all; at least he had never come across one in his days. It was only when he heard the hidden folk mentioned that his ears grew. He somehow knew that he was often being watched even though he was alone in a field, swinging the scythe, or somewhere far from the farm herding the sheep home for milking. Once, when he was a boy, he had been keeping an eye out for a flock of sheep for a farmer he lived with at the time. He was cold and hungry and took shelter under a great rock when the sheep were settled and started to graze happily in the narrow valley where he brought them every day. He fell asleep there, exhausted, and slept for a good time. He was never sure if it was a dream or a memory, but he saw the rock he sat under simply open up, as if there was a door on it, and out came a dozen or so people. He remembered how beautiful they were, how well dressed they were, how happy they seemed and how their rings and bracelets of silver and gold had glistened in the sun. 'One day,' he had thought to himself, 'I am going to be as rich and happy as those folks, and never be hungry or cold again.'

One of the tales told in the dusk that evening was of crossroads. Everyone, including Fúsi, knew that crossroads should be avoided after dark if possible as they are a meeting place of the elves, and whoever meets them seldom returns to tell the tale. One of the young ladies told the story of a fellow who had sat himself down on a crossroads on New Year's Eve and met with the elves. He had become very rich afterwards and nobody knew how exactly. 'This is my chance,' thought Fúsi, quiet in the darkness of his corner as he felted a pair of mittens. 'I will wait for the hidden folks on the crossroads over by the lake on New Year's Eve and become as wealthy as the sheriff. Or even wealthier still!'

The days seemed to crawl by, but finally Yule came with its wonderful meal on the eve before Yule, the only time of the year Fúsi could eat his fill. He could hardly wait and felt as if time had seized up, but Old Year's Eve came and went and it was new year.

He waited for the people to fall quiet all around him. He listened to their breaths deepen and slow down as they fell asleep one by one until he quietly got out of bed, making sure not to wake the little boy who he had to share a bed with. He put on his clothes and walked out of the house, to find a full moon greeting him and lighting up his path. The crossroads were not far off and soon he was sitting down in the middle of them with his heart thumping in his chest. He was not sure whether he was afraid or excited, but tried his best to calm down and waited. He had sat for a good while and had almost nodded off when a pretty, young woman came to him and said, 'Whatever you do Fúsi, do not accept a single thing here tonight. No matter what you are offered, food, cloth, silver or gold, you are to be silent and not accept a single thing. Do this and you will be a wealthy man. I have seen you often before and I know you have lived a hard life, this is your chance. They are coming, I must not be seen!' And with that she was gone in to the moonlight.

The mysterious woman had been right. Scores of people appeared from out of the half-darkness on the crossroads and offered Fúsi such glorious treasures he could not believe existed. There were plates of silver and gold, jewellery covered with coloured stone, clothes fit for a king, everything from pickled sheep bellies to broiled sheep heads, riches and glorious food beyond belief. But Fúsi heeded the advice. He sat quietly in the middle of the crossroads and denied every single item brought before him, and much to his amusement everything he shook his head over was left in a pile that had turned into a heap of gold, food and colour.

After hours of this strange game, he knew it was almost daybreak. Nothing had been brought before him for a while now and all he had to do was wait a bit longer. Then, the last elf came to him. It was a little girl and she held what appeared in the starlight to be a flat, grey plaque. It took him a few moments to realise that she was holding the fat that congeals on top of the water when smoked meat cools down in the pot and it was his favourite thing to eat in the world. 'I was never one to deny the float,' said Fúsi with his mouth watering and his stomach growling. As he took a big bite of the float, he could see the pile in front of him vanish in grey smoke and be whisked away with the morning breeze.

No one knows exactly what happened after that. Fúsi did return to the farm but had lost his mind completely and could not utter a single word nor recognise a single person. He sat on his bed and rowed back and forth, mumbling something no one could make out with a strange expression on his face. All he did from there on was to sit and knit socks, but they were quite good socks.

Mother Dear

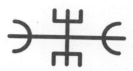

Once upon a time there was a girl named Ólöf. She had lived a difficult life through difficult times. When our story takes place, she was working on a remote farm in the west and knew little but hardship and toil. She had been placed on many farms while growing up, as she was alone in the world, and had learned how to prevail through hunger and pain like so many of her like before her. She had skilled hands and could knit and sew like no one else, something that had caught the attention of the mistress on the farm. When she had finished her chores of milking the cows and ewes and churning the butter each day, her mistress had her sewing the most beautiful aprons and dresses to be sold to the wealthy ladies in the town by the fjord, which felt as far away as the moon. Word had spread about these fine garments and she was worked hard to keep up with demand. She was an unusually pretty girl as well and often felt the eyes of the men around her eagerly following her every move. She went quietly about her ways from day to day, waiting for a better life for herself, where her talents would be hers to benefit from and not the people she was forced to work for.

One winter's evening she heard the other workers on the farm talking between themselves about a secret dance, a gathering arranged by a group of young men in the area that was to take place the following autumn. It was a gathering intended for all the young work folk on the surrounding farms, and they were going to dance a certain dance around a bonfire called Vikivaki. She knew what that was, a round dance with the fire burning in the middle. Hand in hand they would go around and around the fire, singing and laughing, each step bringing them closer together with the flickering lights of the flames guiding them as they danced into the night. It was very much forbidden, that dance, as it was believed to be complete heresy, but she could not wait for time to pass and this became all she could think about.

As the snow thawed and the river by the farm burst free from its icy trap, she was well aware that she did not walk alone any more. Her master's attention towards her, and his frequent and much-dreaded visits to the pantry some weeks before Yule, had created life that she now had to bear with her other burdens. She did her best to conceal that burden as she knew well that, if seen, she would be punished severely and exiled from the farm and not have a single place to go to in this life or anyone to whom she could turn. When her time came, she had to do what so many destitute women had done before her. She crept from her bed one windy night with a single piece of white cloth between her hands and headed for the steep hills above the farm.

The following weeks she was but the shadow of herself. She quietly did her chores, but felt anger and pain in every step and every movement. It was now nearing the end of summer and she spent her days with the ewes as she watched over them and milked them every afternoon. She had carefully watched them as their lambs were separated from them and heard their cries for their offspring, each bleating reaching the deepest nerves in her heart. All she could do was to carry on, even though her weight was almost unbearable.

As nights grew dimmer, she remembered the Vikivaki that had been planned by the spirited young men the autumn before. She knew not whether it would take place or not, but it soon became all she could think about and somehow, she imagined it would become her way out of the cage formed around her heart. Maybe she would meet the man of her dreams and be set free from her life of poverty and toil. One evening, as she had just finished the milking and was about to let the ewes out of the rock-walled pen, she said out loud, although only to herself, 'I have nothing to wear to that dance, I could never attend it.' She then heard the whisper of a child's voice singing, carried to her with the breeze:

> Mother dear in pen, pen,
> Worry not, for when, when.
> I will lend you my white cloth,
> My white cloth to dance in.

As soon as she heard that singing carried by the wind, her heart froze. She saw a veil sweep across her eyes as her awareness left her.

When she woke up the next day she was still lying in the grass outside the pen, wet and cold from the morning dew. She shivered and stumbled like a newborn lamb as she got to her feet and soaked the rays of the morning sun. She mourned for her child as she had done every single day before, but she was determined to dance.

Búkolla

here once lived a man and a woman in their cottage. They had but one son and they did not treat their boy all too well. He was worked very hard and had many chores, and he did all of them without ever a single complaint. He was fed poorly and had to sleep by the hearth, as there was only one bed in the cottage and his parents slept there. He would lay on the cold earth floor and rake pictures in the ashes from the hearth until he fell asleep every night. His hair was thick and grey from the ashes and when he left the house for to fetch water from the creek the wind would blow the ashes around him as if he was standing inside a cloud. Sometimes he thought there could be no one as unlucky as him in the whole world, not even in Orkney. No one knew his name, nor still does, but he was called Karlsson, son of man. Apart from the three of them, there was one more soul in the cottage, that of Búkolla, their cow. She was the centre of their very living; she gave warmth to the tiny house from her stall, she gave them food in their bellies with her milk and to Karlsson she was a friend. He saw in her deep, big eyes, intelligence and warmth and he treated her with the utmost respect and care as he milked her every day, to turn her rich milk into the best of cheese and skyr.

One morning, as usual, the boy got up to do the first milking, while his parents still snored in their bed. Like every morning before, his first glimpse was towards the stall where his friend would greet him with her first deep 'moooo!' of the morning, as if to say, 'Finally my boy, now get over here and do your chores.'

This morning, however, there was no mooing. There was no cow! Not a single trace of his Búkolla, not a splatter of dung, not even a hair on the manger. The boy got up in a hurry and ran outside, looking behind every hill and mound, behind every boulder and cliff, but he could not see so much as a footprint. He dashed back inside to wake up his parents and tell them of their loss. 'What have you done with our cow then boy, you little scoundrel, you waste of space and food, you fool!'

The boy hung his head in sorrow, not because his parents were shouting, no, he had long since stopped paying any attention to that. He cried over his friend Búkolla and in a while said, with a strong voice and his back straight, 'Mother, make me some food for a few days, father make me three new pairs of shoes, for I am going out to find Búkolla.'

To his surprise they did not protest nor did they snort, and with a few looks between them and some faces to go with them, they set about preparing the boy for his search. In those days shoes were made entirely out of leather. The wealthy used tough boots from the hide of bulls, but most often the leather of a lamb was used, even that of a fish. Those would not last too long and the boy somehow suspected he would have to travel far and wide in order to find his cow.

⌖⇻⫛⇺⩺

He set off bright and early the very next day, with food and a couple of new pairs of shoes in a bag in one hand and his walking cane in the other. He chose his direction and on he walked, searching and shouting through fields of lava and hills and lakes, through canyons and heaths. When night fell on the first day, he sat himself down on a broken-down cairn and opened up his pouch. He ate a few bites as the darkness grew thicker and then shouted out in despair and desperation. 'Moo for me Búkolla, if you are anywhere alive!'

His calls were swallowed by the dusk and he felt his loss from the bottom of his heart, when he heard a very faint moooo coming from afar, somewhere very far indeed. He knew it as the voice of his dear Búkolla and swore to find her no matter what lay between them. He got up with the first rays of the sun the next morning and set off in the direction he thought he had heard the mooing.

Karlsson walked and he walked, he waded through mud and snow, crossed rivers and marshes and wore out his shoes. He searched everywhere he could imagine, but there was no sign of the cow. Darkness fell again and he sat himself down on a flat stone surrounded with tall and thick grass and opened up his pouch. He ate a little bit of his food and then shouted again as loud as he could with his spirit lifted by the rest of the skyr he had with him, 'Moo for me Búkolla, if you are anywhere alive!'

He listened hard, into the wind and the wild, holding his breath and could hear his own heart thumping. When he heard a long moo he was sure. 'I am on the right way,' he thought to himself. This time it was much closer and as he put on a new pair of shoes and burrowed himself in the thick grass for the night, he knew he would find Búkolla tomorrow.

Karlsson woke up the next morning before both dawn and sun. Guided by the first rays of the sun, he climbed a tall, steep hill and shouted from the top of his voice, 'Moo for me Búkolla, if you are anywhere alive!'

And right there he could hear her deep voice as her moo bellowed ever so close to him! It took him a while to realise that the noise came from directly beneath his feet. He climbed back down the hill and walked round it until he found an opening to a cave. It was well hidden behind tall grassy banks and was big, very big. As he entered, he saw that the cave was no smaller than its opening suggested, the roof was high enough for a man on a horse to ride around in there and the floor was as wide as a field. Karlsson was curious and began to look around and found the cave to be full of goods. Tools lined the walls, a huge stack of kindling sat next to a burning fire and the two pantries he found were bursting with all manner of delicious food. He could see openings into other caves and fires burning in them as well, riches and goods everywhere he looked. Finally, he found a door that led him in to a smaller room and there he was reunited with his dear Búkolla. Karlsson cried out and the cow let out her loudest noise of joy as he ran into the room and quickly untied her. He held her firmly by a piece of string tied to her bridle and led her out of the cave, not stopping for a moment to grab any of the valuables in the cave.

Once outside, the boy set off home with Búkolla by his side. Well, maybe not so much by his side as behind him. Anyone who has ever tried to lead an Icelandic cow by the halter knows that they can be a handful. They are proud animals and they have their own way and travel at their own speed and not a knot faster. This became clear to Karlsson as he slowly, very slowly, made his way back from where he came from. Much to his horror, as they had only travelled about a quarter of the way, he noticed that they were being followed. Two giant creatures, tall as towers, were on their trail and travelled much faster than the two of them. Karlsson realised these were no ordinary thieves that had taken his cow, but two trolls, and that he had just been in a troll cave. He pulled the string as hard as he could and tried to run but Búkolla just paced on in her usual dramatic tempo, one foot at a time, casually licking her nose every now and then with not a care in the world.

When the trolls had just about caught up with them, Karlsson turned around and looked Búkolla deep in the eyes. He wanted to say something that would get her running, something to get her to speed up, but he could think of nothing. She stared back and somehow the boy felt relieved. 'What are we to do now my dear Búkolla,' said the boy in anguish and much to his amazement and terror she replied!

'Pluck a hair from my tail, boy, and place it on the ground!' She then turned to the hair laying on the ground and spoke again! 'I so say and do demand, that you will turn into a loch, so vast and wide that no one will ever get around it but the bird that soars.'

With his jaw dropping, absolutely flabbergasted, the boy watched as the earth shipped and shifted and a loch as big as the sea itself was created before his eyes. Búkolla gave him a single look and with great care, thrust her tongue far up her left nostril. She then set off home again in her usual calm manner with the boy behind her not believing anything he had just seen.

As the two trolls came to the shores of this new, gigantic loch, they were furious, to say the least. The older one grunted through her teeth, 'This will not do you any good boy,' then turned to the younger one and snarled, 'Run home, you, and fetch me your father's biggest bull!'

The little one, who was anything but little, ran off and the big one sat down grinding her teeth. The little one did return with her father's biggest bull in a short while, and it was a very big bull. It could easily have filled up the great hall of a mighty castle, should any Icelander have seen the inside of a castle. Its head almost touched the clouds above and as the big troll-wife led it to the waterline it began to drink. It drank and it drank, and the water guzzled into its massive mouth with all manner of fish and weed being sucked along, filling its mighty guts until it looked like an enormous blue whale stranded on the beach. With all the water drunk by the big bull, the two trolls set off again, this time even angrier and more malicious.

Karlsson could soon, too soon, see the pair approaching them again. This time he did not try in any way to speed up his trusted companion but instead tried his luck the second time. 'What are we to do now my dear Búkolla?' he asked her as he gazed into her eyes, like they were those of a girl he once met after mass on Sunday and could never fully stop thinking about.

'Pluck a hair from my tail, boy, and place it on the ground!' Again the wise cow turned to the hair on the ground. 'I so say and demand that you will turn in to a fire, so big that no one will ever get over it but the bird that soars.'

And with that, the hair caught fire and the fire grew and grew until it burned as big and hot and fierce as only an erupting volcano can burn. The boy jumped up and down with joy, certain that the trolls would never be able to put out something as magnificent as that fire. This time, Búkolla thoroughly cleaned out her right nostril before heading home again.

This was of no liking to the two trolls. As they reached the fire, the older one spat at it and said, 'This will not do you any good, boy!' To the little one she growled, 'Run back, you, and fetch that bull again!'

She spat in the fire again as she stared into it with a frown on her face, muttering no nice things about the boy. This time it took a bit longer to fetch the bull, as it was quite heavy from drinking all that water and marine life. It waddled behind the smaller troll, leaving deep footprints behind, and could hardly take another step when they finally reached the fire.

'About time!' roared the troll-wife as she grabbed the bull by the horn and aimed it at the fire. As she did so the bull pissed all the water it had drunk right into the fire. The thick, dark yellow liquid oozed from the animal, which let out a sigh of relief and the stench that rose as the fire was put out was unbearable. Grass and flowers wilted all around, stones cracked in half, but the trolls could not smell a thing and only rejoiced over their luck and wit. And off they went again, leaving a very confused bull behind.

For the third time now, Karlsson noticed the two trolls following them. He could not for the life of him understand how the two trolls managed to get over that wall of fire and wondered what strange smell was being carried through the breeze. This time around he was both confident and sure of himself, or rather his wonderful cow. He turned to her and with almost a grin on his face he said, 'What are we to do now my dear Búkolla?'

With her mighty eyes she looked at the boy and for a second he felt as if the animal in front of him bore the wisdom of a thousand ages. 'Pluck a hair from my tale, boy, and place it on the ground!' She turned gracefully to the hair and said, 'I so say and demand that you will turn in to a mountain, so high and coarse that no one will ever get over it but the soaring bird.'

From the hair small piles of stone began to tumble and then it was as if the ground split to let out a sigh, but instead of a sigh, a mountain grew in front of them. It was enormous, the boy could not see the top of it, no matter how hard he looked, and its roots seemed to stretch over the whole of the land. He looked to his cow in awe as she turned around for home. She gave a flicker with her tail and sent off a speck of dung from earlier that day, straight on the boy's cheek.

When the two trolls reached the foot of the mountain set in their path they both went absolutely berserk. They ground their teeth, roared and grunted and cursed the boy in all manner possible. 'This will do you no good boy!' screamed the pair of them, and the big one then shouted at the little one that was not small in any way, 'Go home you little twerp and fetch your father's big drill and be quick about it!'

With that the little one left her mother by the newly formed mountain in a marvellous fit of rage and ran back to the cave. She ran both ways, back and forth, and that is saying something, holding that drill. It was as big as a house that drill. Not a house like Karlsson lived in with his cow and his parents, no, it was as big as one of the houses he had seen in the town by the sea, where the goods were kept that came from the ships. The big, angry troll-wife grabbed the drill and with a great effort and a few grunts, she began drilling through the mountain. She drilled and she drilled, sparks flew in all direction from the drill as it gnawed its way through the bedrock and her sweat ran in creeks from where she was standing. In as long as it takes a fox to eat its fill she drilled all the way through. She jammed her head in the gaping hole and yelled profanities after the boy who, much to his concern, could hear them quite clearly. The two trolls than crawled into the hole and started clawing their way through the mountain. On they crawled, metre by metre and soon they were almost all the way through. They made their final effort and as the pair of them were about to squeeze their ugly heads out the other side, the sun came out in all its glory and bathed the land in its gold. There are not many things as spectacular as the sun rising, blood red and big, on an Icelandic spring morning, as we all know, but the only thing not pleased with the sun are the trolls. Every child knows that when the sun shines on a night troll it is turned to stone, and that was exactly what became of the two trolls in the mountain.

Karlsson and Búkolla found their way home to the cottage and found his parents worried out of their mind, not only for Búkolla but for their boy as well. From then on, and every day after, they treated him with love and respect and he grew up to be a man of wit and strength. He made his way to the cave shortly after his adventure with Búkolla and on the way he found a gigantic rock, just by the opening where the two trolls had turned to stone. It had the shape of someone very, very big and was hunched as if it was looking in the hole for one reason or the other. From the cave Karlsson brought home with him all manner of riches, tools and livestock and other glorious items to ease the burden of his daily life. I will call this enough about the boy Karlsson, but add that Búkolla became the oldest and happiest of cows, never uttered another word and ate but the best hay till her last day.

Now, if you visit Iceland on your travels, you know the story of why the Icelandic highlands seem to be one soaring, vast, endless mountain.

The Scythe

My great-grandmother, Guðfríður, lived on the same farm where we live today. It is named Litla Brekka and is on the west coast of the country. It is a very good farm to farm sheep, with plentiful grazing, creeks running through the land and fields that grow thick and green grass. My family has bred sheep and horses and harvested that land for five generations, and you might say we know our way around the farm by now. Guðfríður came from a small farm named Gufuá, but moved when she married my great-grandfather, Guðmundur. Her sister, Ásta, moved away as well, but she went all the way to America to find a better life for herself. Her descendants can tell us all about her adventures over there. Together Guðmundur and Guðfríður built up a big farm and were hard working, well off and honest people. They had YYY children but lost three of them at a very young age and one daughter at the age of 30. Life can be as cruel as it can be rewarding and my great-grandparents got to experience both sides.

Guðfríður was a midwife. Truth be told, we do not

have the word midwife in our language but a different
one, 'ljósmóðir' or 'lightmother', the mother of light. I am
not sure if a more beautiful, fitting and descriptive word
could have been chosen for this particular profession, but
my great-grandmother was a lightmother. She was the
only qualified lightmother in the region where we live
and was used to being brought to help women give birth
in all weathers and conditions all year round. She was a
very good rider and always made sure she had good, well-
trained horses at hand on her farm, as she was a farmer
alongside my great-grandfather, as well as delivering light.
Her career was a successful one, to say the least, as she did
not lose a single baby, despite working in often very primitive conditions, as every woman at the time would give
birth at home. This meant that Guðfríður would ride with
whoever was sent to bring her, and then make the most of
what was at hand in the house, as well as her equipment
that she brought with her in a leather case. After the birth,
she would then spend a day or so in the house to make sure
the mother and child would fare well before riding home to
Guðmundur. He, very much against the norm at the time,
did not at all mind caring for their own little children and
changed nappies and fed babies as gently as he delivered
lambs in the spring. I am told they loved books and poetry,
had a strong relationship and that they never quarrelled.
In fact. Guðmundur came home one day from the town
where he had been running errands, something that was
not done very often, and was beautifully drunk. 'Are you
drunk, my dear?' asked Guðfríður as she saw the state of
her husband and he replied, 'As drunk as I deserve to be.'
And that was that.

There once was a lightmother who lived on a farm.
She was a good lightmother, lucky and skilled and could

ride in any weather to the aid of women in the neighbourhood giving birth. She was well known for her skill, and she was also well known for her strong connection with nature and all that grows. She could blend ointments that healed the worst of wounds and she could brew potions that took the mind away from any pain. She had never lost a child and could turn a baby in the womb to deliver it safely into the world and knew every trick in the book. Her husband was a good man, able and strong, and a very good farmer. He was an excellent blacksmith, his knives and scythes were as sharp as a mountain's edge and his tools sturdy and strong. His barns were filled with hay, his sheep were many and they were big and the lambs that fell in the autumn were the fattest in the region. The two of them had a few horses, white as snow and taller than the usual you see all around the country and as strong as oxen. As if this luck and abundance wasn't enough, their dog was known all around the west. Some people said it was the best sheepdog in all of the west, and they were probably very right to say so. Left and right round the flock it would go on a single command, it would stop and return a stray ewe before being ordered so and it could run almost endlessly while gathering and herding.

One afternoon, in the middle of summer, the couple were out in one of their fields cutting grass. They swung their scythes in a perfect rhythm and the grass lay before their feet in neat rows to be dried and then raked together before being brought home and inside for the winter. The sun was shining and they were working hard and felt tired, happy and hungry. After a good while of swinging the scythes, they decided it was time for a wee break. They sat down next to each other in the field, carefully placing the scythes with the blade facing up so that none of their children, who were playing merrily around them, would cut themselves on the sharp blade unseen in the tall grass. They opened up a bag and began to feast on a particularly fat liver sausage and drank milk with it.

The dog, never far off from his masters, could smell something very appealing close by, whether he could smell the fat sausage, or a fancy bitch in heat somewhere in the distance, we will never know, but it ran. And my, did it run. Like an arrow from a hunter's bow, it soared through the air getting ever closer and closer to his masters, who by now were on their feet yelling, waving and screaming, but to no avail. The poor creature ran right on to one of the scythes and was split in half, with each half dropping on its side on the ground. The lightmother had her quick wits about her this day, as all the others. She grabbed the two halves, as quick as a sheep changes its mind, and slammed them together. She then ran with all her might in the house to work her wonders, with her husband sobbing behind her. When he finally reached the house and found his way in, he was met with a very strange sight indeed. His wife had tightly wound a piece of linen around and around and around the dog, leaving nothing unwrapped except the tip of the snout and the other end that needs certain freedom towards the open air. She then took some of her remedies and poured them over the tightly wrapped bundle, and perhaps even spoke a few quiet words to strengthen the deed. The poor creature was alive in the bundle, that was for sure as the tongue wiggled from the end and the mouth happily accepted food. The other end soon began to produce, so the dog was obviously healing well.

Days turned to weeks, and it was autumn. It was now

time for the annual highland herding of the sheep, or 'the searches' as the event is called in our region. That is when the farm people of a certain area come together and ride together towards a hut in the mountains and stay there for a few days, as the sheep that have been left grazing there the whole summer are rounded up. This is a pattern followed through generations and has not changed much for hundreds of years. It is a time people look forward to, as much as it can get difficult, but to ride with friends and neighbours in the Icelandic mountains for a few days with a flask by your belt, running after some of the most stubborn creatures ever to roam the land, and spectacular views in front of you, is an experience no one forgets. This time though, the farmer prepared himself in silence and with a sad look turned his eye to the bundle now laying in his bed.

'Try him out, I believe it's time,' said the lightmother to her husband.

That was all he needed. With a wide smile he began to unwrap his beloved friend and found a tail. Then a hind leg, and another hind leg, but his smile soon dimmed. Something was not right. As he finished his unravelling he saw that two of the animal's feet, the left ones to be precise, were facing downwards but the right ones up! His skilled and quick wife had slammed the halves together upside down in all the haste to save the poor thing.

'Bring him anyway,' said the lightmother, and with a frown the farmer set off with his odd-looking dog, running and jumping merrily around him, obviously feeling on the top of the world.

When the people met to set off, the pair of them were met with roars of laughter. 'What have you got there my friend, a spider!?'

'And to think you used to have the best one of us all!'

The farmer did his best to laugh along with the jokes, but in fact he felt awful and ashamed. Off the lot of them rode and soon, as the singing began and the flasks found their way between the folks, the farmer found his smile and good spirits. Suddenly a small flock of sheep was startled by the singing and laughter from the riders and scampered from under a cliff in to the surrounding hills. The dog took one look and was off. And off it was indeed. The people watched in disbelief as the dog ran like the wind on two feet, with the other two sticking out like branches from a tree. It caught the sheep in an instant and brought them back, running to its master for a pat on the head as if nothing had ever happened. The search went well and the sheep were rounded up and brought home to the farms, as tradition has it.

The farmer was beside himself, what a dog he had still. If anyone had thought the dog to be the best one in the west, it was now without a shadow of a doubt the best dog in the whole country. After all, how many dogs do you know that can jump on to another set of feet once it grows tired of running after misbehaving ewes?

In Need

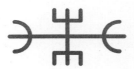

Just a stone's throw away from a small house nestled between mountains there stood a hillock, green and lush. It was a place where children played and sheep grazed, but the farmers there had not cut the grass on it for generations. No one was exactly sure why that was. It was, as said before, covered in lush green grass and would have provided quite a lot of hay, but no one dared to, as it was simply forbidden by the old people at each time. One old lady living on the farm could tell a story though, and she could tell it first hand, so to speak. She and a group of children had been playing in the steep hills when they had found a small opening in the grass. For a while the group had played innocently enough, pretending to reach into the opening for toys and other wonders. Eventually one of the youngest, a sweet little girl, had put her hand in and sang in her pretty voice, 'Lay some good in hand, hand, nothing will I see, see.'

When she pulled out her hand she held a shining silver button in it, the most beautiful thing the children had ever seen. The oldest of the children happened to be the old lady telling the story and she got carried away by the beauty of that button. She shoved the little girl out of the way, stuck her own hand in and sang the same little line. She screamed as she pulled out her hand, withered and lifeless, as it remained for the rest of her days. The people believed her story as she had the withered hand to prove it and children were told to play with respect and the grass was never cut.

One night in the midst of Þorri, the coldest and darkest of the old months, Áshildur, the key holder on the farm, was lying in her bed trying to get some sleep. Her day in the pantry, churning butter and making cheese, had been a long one, and was followed by a long night of knitting by a single lamp. Her cow was milking very well these days, unusually well, and she therefore had a lot of milk to turn into food. Even though, she could not find sleep, nor would sleep find her and she stared into the darkness as she tried to calm her mind. Her young husband lay beside her like a dead man, apart from the occasional snore. Suddenly, she could hear the front door opened by the end of the tunnel. She quietly lay, holding her breath. She was just about to wake her husband, as she heard footsteps in the dark, when she heard a voice whisper her own name. 'Can you help me neighbour?' whispered the voice, 'I have done your cow well over the past weeks because I thought I might need your help soon. I know that you are a woman of wisdom and my wife needs help. Do not deny me this.'

Against her will and better judgement, Áshildur got quietly to her feet and followed the visitor outside. She knew it could be no one from the area, as they lived remotely and far away from the next farms. The moon was full and snow covered the ground, so she could easily make out a tall and very handsome man in front of her. 'Follow me please,' he whispered and took her hand.

They walked towards the hillock she knew so well as she had played on the slopes herself as a child. This time it looked nothing like a hillock, but a beautiful farmhouse with bright light streaming from many windows. They entered through a tall doorway and were soon by the bedside of a beautiful woman in labour. 'Something is wrong and I cannot deliver,' said the woman in agony. 'I know that you have helped women before and I know you can help me.'

Áshildur felt the woman's belly and was soon giving orders in a relaxed, yet driven manner. 'Hot water and linen,' she said. 'Strong ale and a sharp knife.'

All this was provided by the man of the house and the ale went down well to ease pain and stress for both ladies. Incredibly soon the woman in the bed had given birth to a healthy and big baby boy, who screamed at the top of his lungs in the face of his very relieved father. Áshildur watched in wonder as the man sat down with his son in his arms and gently applied a wonderful-smelling ointment on to his son's eyes. The aroma of a thousand flowers filled the room and the boy cooed gently in his father's lap. He was so mesmerised by his son that he did not notice as Áshildur quickly reached for the jar and helped herself to a little bit of that wondrous ointment. If it was good for a baby's eye and smelled so good, it could hardly do her own eye any harm. She applied it in haste to her right eye and continued her work in the house. She was startled as she could now see several people in the house, young and old, all with the same expression of relief and joy on their pretty faces. As the night wore on the woman recovered remarkably fast. She was soon on her feet with the baby fed and fast asleep in his cot and her husband beaming, tending to her every need.

'Thank you. I am not sure if this would have gone so well without you,' said the man as he led the lady to the door to see her off. 'Your cow will continue to milk well for the rest of her days, as will your others as well.

'I have but the one,' Áshildur replied as the man shook her hand with a strange smile.

'We will not see each other again, but luck will follow you,' he said and closed the door behind her.

It was near dawn when she closed her eyes beside her husband and fell fast asleep. When she woke up late that morning she was not sure if she had saved a woman and child or had a strange dream. She went through her routine and her work as every other morning, still with the aroma from the ointment on her senses. It was not until she bowed herself through the doorway to the cow shed that she was sure. Beside her red cow now stood another grey one, young and pretty with its udder bursting with milk. It was well after midday that Áslaug had the time to leave the house for some well-earned winter sun and fresh air. Instead of her beloved hillock she now saw as clear as day the house she had been inside the night before. She could see people around the house and through the windows, very much like her own family going about their daily life. She did not show the slightest sign of noticing them though, and when her husband and children came home from feeding the sheep she had no answer as to why they now had a new cow in the shed.

Over the next few years Áshildur became well known for her knowledge and eccentricity, as she somehow seemed to have a deeper understanding of life's many aspects than others. She could foresee whether when hay was harvested and had incredible luck with breeding and farming. She invented tools and methods, and she became a well-known lightmother, who never lost a child. One day, many years later when she was an old woman, she saw the man from that fateful evening on a street in the closest town. Much as herself he was old and worn but still had that strong and proud look about him. She let her guard down for a second and stopped in front of him with a smile.

'Hello friend, how are you. How wonderful it has been to see your son grow up and become the handsome man he is today. He is such a hard worker. I am sorry for your loss though, I saw your wife's kist taken to her burial a few weeks ago. I guess we are getting quite old.'

Without a single word the old man put his thumb in his mouth and then stroked it across Áshildur's right eye. She felt a sharp pain and he was gone from her sight. When she came home later that evening she could make out the green, lush hillock she remembered so well, but no house. She had lost the sight in her right eye and felt both years older and a deep regret for the world she could no longer see.

The Hallowing of Látrabjarg

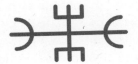

átrabjarg is a tremendous cliff that rises from the Atlantic like a giant of ancient times. In fact, that is exactly what it is, a giant of ancient times. It greeted the first sailors to approach the west fjords, as it has greeted the birds that rest in its crevasses and sills for centuries upon centuries. It seems to stretch endlessly along the coast, with the waves constantly pounding it, keeping its feet wet at all time. It is the most western tip of the country, one of the points from where the giant Bull of the West peers out on to the vast ocean as he defends the country. He is one of the four mighty beings set to protect the land along with the Eagle in the North, the Dragon in the East and the Giant in the South. These protectors of the land, along with great many more of all shapes and sizes, were what met the wizard sent to Iceland in the form of a whale by King Harald of Norway when he wanted to conquer the land. The wizard, still hopefully in the form of a whale if he was not a very strong swimmer himself, returned to King Harald with this news, to his little delight. When ships approached this land in earlier times, the dragon heads that adorned the ships, and led the way, were to be removed from the bow so as not to anger these protectors, such was the respect paid to them. Sadly, dragonheads are rarely seen on ships these days, but Látrabjarg still soars over the rocky shore and the restless sea below, home to countless seabirds of all types and to their eggs and their young.

After a particularly long and harsh winter, the people of Látrar were facing a terrible problem. The farm relied heavily on the gathering of eggs on Látrabjarg for food, even though the sea provided them with fish as well. This particular spring something awful was afoot. The ropes of braided strips of cow hide that were used to lower people over the cliff were being cut while lowering those gathering eggs. Two men had lost their lives as they fell into the sea, or to the beach below, and deep sadness loomed over the farm. Because of this, no one dared to gather eggs and the people were frustrated and hungry. One afternoon, three young fellows from a neighbouring farm arrived at the doorstep, having heard about the troubles. They were no strangers to gathering eggs from the cliff and had with them their own ropes, 'the strongest in the land', as they said, and they did not believe a single word about a fiend on the cliff cutting ropes. 'Obviously, these poor folks are using rotted out ropes, or they are doing it wrong and cutting the ropes on the sills,' they boasted, filled with the wonderful stupidity that can only blossom in the hearts of young men who believe they own the world. Despite strong objection from the farmer, they set off to the tip of the cliff and prepared to lower one of them down.

ᛟᚦ᛫ᚻᛁᛁᛁᚦᛁᚴᚴ

The young man was fearless, and the last his friends saw of him was the smirk on his face as he climbed over the edge with the gaping void beneath him. He was the oldest of the three and the other two let out the rope on his command and could hear him shouting, 'There are plenty of eggs and nothing foul down here at all, I have almost got a full pouch already! Bring me a bit lower, boys, I am going to sit myself down on a sill further down and fill the pouch!'

Soon he was more than halfway down the cliff and they could hardly hear him anymore. The rope slackened and the two waited for the tug on the rope that told them to pull their friend up. 'Do you think we should pull him up,' asked the younger of the two, 'I cannot hear him anymore, can you?'

'No, but you are right, he has been down there a good while.'

Just as they let off those words, they felt a long tug and pulled on the rope. Much to their horror it soon felt as if they were pulling up air and all they brought up was the rope. It had been cut, just as they had been warned. They returned with what was left of the rope and their belongings and told their story at Látrar with a heavy heart.

An old man lived out the last of his life in Látrar at the same time. He was seen by the farm folk to be but a burden that only took up space and food and nobody knew his story, nor had bothered to ask. He had been completely blind for years and could hardly move without help. He heard the boys' story and with a weak and trembling voice he asked to hold the cut rope. The farmer reluctantly reached for the rope and gave it to the old man, with a frown on his face. The old man held the end in front of him and for a second it seemed as he could see once more, when the cloud lifted from his eyes. He sniffed the rope and felt the end with his fingers, and somehow looked years younger for a moment before saying, 'This rope was cut by two. Two strands of the rope were cut by a foe of some sorts, but one was cut by a man. I suggest you head back to the cliff and lower another rope at the same spot and see what you find.' The boys, as well as the rest of the household, looked in surprise at the old withered man in the corner and thought to themselves that maybe they had been a little too quick to pass their judgement.

The farmer and the boys quickly made their way to the cliff and lowered a new rope on the same spot as before. The three of them sat on the edge of the cliff and exchanged worried looks between them, half wishing that there would be a tug on the rope and half wishing there would not. Sure enough though, when the rope was almost out full length, they felt the tug and began to hoist whatever was down there upwards. It was hard to see who was the most relieved when the third boy appeared over the edge of the cliff, the boy who had been stranded or the three pulling the rope.

'What happened down there,' said the farmer, 'tell me now boy!'

'As I was sitting on a big ledge low in the cliff, holding the rope for support, I saw a great, big arm reaching out of a cleft just above my head. It held a knife and sliced the rope until it had severed two of the three strands. I knew the one left would not carry my weight, so I cut that one myself. That was a hard thing to do,' said the boy, immensely glad to have his feet on solid ground. The farmer took the three boys home and fed them well before sending them off home.

o>III>I<

Soon, the word about this evil in the cliff and what had happened, reached every farm and village in the area. People were frightened and avoided the cliff, fearing that whatever was haunting it could find its way to the top and do them harm, or even throw them into the abyss below. A while had passed when a man, unknown to the people of Látrar, knocked on the door one evening and asked to stay for a night and be fed. As was the custom of the time, travellers could somewhat depend on getting a meal and a bed at farms they came across, though the hospitality could vary quite a lot from one farm to the other. The man was invited into the house and given a space in an old man's bed and a bowl of food to eat. As the stranger sat quietly on the bed and ate, the old man raised himself with great effort and looked at the man.

'We need your help, and I know you can give it,' he said in his weak voice.

'I know your troubles and I have come to see what I can do,' replied the man, but he did not utter a single word more after that. He finished his meal and lay down next to the old man and fell asleep. The next morning, he was gone when the people woke up at dawn.

'A great good he did us,' mumbled the farmer as he ate his morning's bowl of porridge and left for his daily work.

The stranger had indeed got up before anyone else, but was now out on the cliff, walking the long way from end to end. He clutched his walking stick, stayed as near the edge as he could and muttered something the whole time, so low that it barely left his lips. He reached the spot where the boy had been stranded and stopped in his tracks. His muttering became louder and his face hardened, until the massive form of a man came climbing over the edge. He was as big as a house and had long, black hair down his back. His dark eyes shot sparks over a beard so thick and course it looked like a raven's nest. He spoke in a deep voice that shook the ground beneath them.

'Stop your hallowing, whoever you are, the wicked need their place in the world as well! Here I live with all of my folk and have done for as long as this land has stood. Every day I row my boat out into the waters below, along with eleven others, and each boat seats twelve of us. Each one has twelve lines with twelve hooks, and we catch shark and seal, cod and haddock. That should tell you a little something about how many of us there are to feed!'

The man looked down to the ground after this speech for a while and was silent. He then looked the giant man in the eye and nodded once. With that he turned his back and kept walking, and did so until he reached the end of Látrabjarg.

The stranger returning that same evening was the last thing the people in Látrar expected. He knocked on the door, as the night before, and the farmer answered.

'I have made the cliff safe again for your people, farmer, all except where the boys had their troubles. No one shall ever again be lowered into that part of the cliff as it is not yours anymore.'

He turned around and was gone into the night without a single goodbye. The very next day the farmer and two with him set off to the cliff with new ropes and their pouches. They were hesitant, to say the least, but curious as well and lowered the farmer down as so many times before. In a short while he gave the tug on the rope that told the people to haul him up again and brought up a pouch full of eggs. That evening the people of Látrar ate their fill of eggs for the first time in a long while, and soon others were making good use of the thousands and thousands of nests in the cliff as well. For a very long time, however, nobody came so much as close to the spot where the stranger had met the giant man. It was considered a very dangerous place, and some say to this day it should not be approached. That part of the cliff was named Heiðnabjarg, or 'Heathen cliff', and holds that name still today.

The Laughing Merman

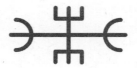

On Reykjanes peninsula the towns and villages are many. That is no wonder, since it is the perfect place to row from towards some very fine fishing grounds. Those grounds have been known and fished since the settlement of this island in the Atlantic and knowledge of them passed from one generation to the other. One fine morning in one of these villages, a young fisherman was getting his boat ready for a day of fishing. A village is hardly the name for it though, in fact there were only a few houses scattered along the beach and some of the settlers even still living in their tents. The young man was recently married and he knew the other fellows envied him endlessly. There was no doubt that his beautiful wife was the most wonderful lass in the whole of the land and he still could not believe his fortune. The two of them had just finished building a little cottage for themselves on a small hillock by the shore and made sure to have room for a cot should the gods bless them.

The sun was shining and the sea was calm that day, and the young man rowed until he caught a nice breeze

and set sail. Life was wonderful. He soon made it to his
favourite spot and lowered the line he had baited the
night before. Bits of herring on newly made iron hooks
disappeared one by one into the depths of the Atlantic
and soon all of them were dangling in front of yellow,
hungry cod. He tied the line to a hook and as he kept the
boat in the same spot with the oars out, his mind began
to wander as it always did. If he kept spending every day
fishing as he had done since the house was built, he could
soon afford a bigger boat. Then he would hire a couple of
lads to man that boat with him and if the gods smiled he
could get another one with another crew. He was in the
middle of these ponderings when he felt a great, big pull
on the line. It was such a yank that the boat nearly tipped
over and the fisherman grabbed the side with both hands.
'This is big!' he thought to himself and hoped for a skate.
Or a monster of a halibut. Or even a shark! Whatever it
was he had caught it was big and he began to pull in the
line and knew that he would make a good sale when he
reached the village. He pulled and he pulled until he saw
a dark, big shadow approaching the surface of the water.
It was big indeed and he felt uneasy as the form drew
nearer. As he heaved the great lump of flesh into the boat
he gasped in awe.

What now sat opposite the young seamen was
something he recognised immediately. His father and
grandfather had told him all the old stories and he knew
every critter of the sea. A merman and nothing else was
glaring angrily at him from the opposite thwart with a
look of utter dismay upon his face. 'What an endlessly
rude thing to do!' the merman said in a shrill voice. 'There
I was, happily climbing my mother's chimney to get rid
of a soot block for the old lady when I was yanked away

with a great, big hook and dragged to the retched surface. What sort of manners are they?'

He was obviously furious and the young fisherman could not help but to feel a little bit ashamed. He looked down for a moment but then took a deep breath. 'Now you listen to me!' he said in his deepest voice. 'I am a fishermen as was my father before me and his father before him! Whatever I catch in the sea I keep and I am keeping you for sure!' For what purpose though he was not quite sure yet. He angrily grabbed hold of the oars and began to row towards shore as the wind did not move a hair on his head. The merman snorted and crossed his arms and the silence was thick.

Whatever else could be said about the young fishermen, he could never stay angry for long. About halfway home he tried to engage in conversation with the merman. He asked him about his mother, about how the houses looked down in the depths, if there were many of his kind and so on. When the merman did not even so much as look at him, he began to tell about his new house, his lovely wife, the slowly forming village and the voyage to the new land. Not a sound could be heard from the merman so the young man soon gave up. He rowed in silence until his boat touched shore. He jumped out of the boat and looked at his catch, which did not look back.

'How stubborn can one creature be,' he mumbled as he lifted the merman out of the boat and set him down on the beach as if he was a child. 'If this is how you want to play, I do not care anymore what you do with yourself. I am going home to see my beautiful wife and have a bite to eat.'

As soon as he had spoken those words, he turned around and was met by his dog, who had come running from home as fast as the little legs would carry him when he had felt his master's scent and seen his boat. Frantically wagging the tail and drooling with joy, the dog jumped the young man with filthy paws and wet fur. 'Get off me you filthy mutt!' he shouted as he threw the dog down. He then gave the poor thing a kick and began to stroke away the dirt left on his shirt.

'Ha ha ha ha,' the merman's laughter rang like a bell as he pointed and laughed at the young man. 'Ha ha ha,' he laughed and laughed until finally stopping with a great grin on his face.

'What are you laughing at then? Do you think I enjoy a greeting like that, getting my new shirt all filthy and all? My wife made it for me to wear at sea!'

The merman did not utter a single word in response. The fisherman strode off with a badly bruised ego. He turned around and said angrily, 'I am going home. If you care to join me then join me, but frankly I do not care anymore what happens to you.'

As he walked off, the merman stood still for a few seconds but then smiled to himself. He followed the young man and watched his every move.

The walk to the hillock where the new house stood was not far. Already there was a little footpath winding from the shore up to the house and the young fisherman was about halfway up the path when he stubbed his toe on a wee mound in the grass and fell face flat in to a fresh splatter of dung, carefully and recently left there by his own cow. He had often thought of fetching a shovel to dig that little mound out of the path but now all he could do was give it a great kick as he cussed between his clenched teeth and a good portion of cow dung. 'Ha ha ha ha ha!' the merman laughed hard and loud. 'Ha ha ha ha,' he laughed and even pointed like a little boy would, at the awful misfortune of our hero. This time the young man just gave the merman an angry stare before striding up the hill and through the little gate into his little garden.

His anger melted away like the thinnest snow before spring sun when his wonderful wife came out of the house. She was as pretty as the spring sun indeed, and she opened her arms and hugged her husband and kissed him the deepest kiss.

'Ha ha ha ha ha,' the merman roared, 'ha ha ha ha ha,' but the young man hardly noticed. He was in another place, above and beyond himself, and could perceive little but the sweetest of kisses. When he came to, the merman was still snorting. 'Aha, ha ha, hmmm,' he quietly laughed as he stroked tears out of his eyes.

'Listen you. I will make you a deal. If you spend the night with me and my wife in our house and share a meal and a blether, I will take you back out tomorrow and set you free in the very spot I caught you earlier today. But only if you tell me why you laughed at me!'

The merman smiled again and looked the fisherman in the eye. 'Deal,' he said and followed the young couple into the house. To make a long story short, not that we would ever want that, the three of them had a wonderful time. They ate well and they drank well, they had many things in common and the dark ale did them justice into the deep night.

They woke up the next morning and the fisherman said as they ate their breakfast, 'I will be sorry to see you go merman.'

'Worry not my friend, good things await you. Now take me home.'

And that he did. They caught a strong breeze and were far out in a short time. 'Here we are then,' said the fisherman, 'are you going to tell me then?'

'Of course I am. As we touched shore yesterday, your dog came running to greet you, remember? No being, animal, man or woman has ever loved you as unconditionally as that dog does, nor ever will. It waits for your arrival every day and welcomes you with the purest heart imaginable. And what did you do? You kicked it. Perhaps you should pay better attention to those who truly love you. Of course I laughed at you. You are an imbecile.

Now, for the second time. Are you so arrogant to think that you are the first to come to this land and settle? Do you think no one lived before you or your fathers? You are but a link in a chain my friend. Inside that mound in your footpath is a chest. It contains a hoard of silver left there a very long time ago by your own people and patiently awaits to be dug out. Perhaps you should look better where you tread. When you kicked your own fortune, well, of course I laughed. You are an imbecile.

Well. That third time I laughed. You see my good man, your wife is truly beautiful and your house is too but you are not the only one to notice that. In fact, when your friend the blacksmith stops by when you are out fishing to leave those fish hooks he makes for you, well, that is not all he leaves behind. Perhaps you should look closer to yourself. Of course I laughed. You are an imbecile. Now sail back home my friend and find your fortune!'

And with that the merman dove into the water, hardly leaving a splash, let alone a wave.

The fisherman had no rest in his bones to fish that day. He sailed home and made sure to lovingly pet his dog as he pulled his boat ashore. His heart was pounding in his chest as he kneeled by the little mound in the path to his home and revealed from within a small but beautifully ordained larch chest. As promised, it was full of silver coins and bracelets and stones of deepest colours. He found his friend the blacksmith, but that is a story we need not delve into here as this is a happy tale and our last one for now.

He did, however, find something else, something quite peculiar. Behind his house he saw seven cows. They were gloriously fat, big and grey like the thickest fog and their udders were big and full of milk. Each one had a great, red balloon growing out of its nose and, knowing all the lore surrounding the sea, he knew what those were. They were sea cows, the best cows in the whole world, and he also knew exactly what to do next. He grabbed his great-grandfather's staff from where it hung in the hallway of his now empty house and ran towards the cows. He moved quickly but only managed to pop the balloon on three of the cows before the rest of them reached the beach and disappeared with great splashes into the waves. The three though were as calm as snails and happily followed their new master home. His late mother's red cow happily greeted the three and the young fisherman could hardly believe his own fortune.

And this is the story about how grey cows came to live in Iceland.